THE MEMORY BOX

Kay Correll

Published by Rose Quartz Press

ISBN-13: 978-0-9904822-3-9

This book is dedicated to my five boys. You drive me crazy, make me laugh, give meaning to my life.
You are my favorite.

COMFORT CROSSING ~ THE SERIES

The Shop on Main - Book One
The Memory Box - Book Two
The Christmas Cottage - A Holiday Novella (Book 2.5)
The Letter - Book Three
The Christmas Scarf - A Holiday Novella (Book 3.5)
The Magnolia Cafe - Book Four
The Unexpected Wedding - Book Five

Chapter One

Jenny Bouchard dropped a quarter in the jukebox at the Magnolia Cafe. She stared at the plastic button labeled B19. The button she always avoided. The song on B19 hadn't changed in over twenty years.

She stood there ignoring B19... *really she was.* Her mind flooded with memories. She could almost feel Clay Miller's physical presence beside her, taking her hand, transporting her back in time to the days of secret meetings and stolen moments together. So long ago. She tried so hard to push those memories from all consciousness. They should have been long forgotten, but occasionally she couldn't fight it any longer, and they came rushing back, riding on waves of emotion.

Jenny's heart tightened in her chest. For a moment, she sucked in air, but it didn't seem to fill her lungs. So many choices she'd made, so many forks in the road, with impossible decisions to make. When neither option was one she had wanted to choose. But life was like that. And all those choices had led her to where she was now. She couldn't change the path she had taken, but every once in a while she couldn't help playing "what if." Even if the game of "what if" was a slow, melancholy torture.

She closed her eyes and let the memories engulf her. She could almost smell the scent of Clay's aftershave. Feel the closeness of him. Relive the feeling of completeness and safety in his arms.

"Hey, Jenns." The voice was low. Deep. Warm. She almost believed she had really heard him. The memories were sucking her back in time, playing tricks with her mind.

"Jenns?"

That sounded more real. She opened her eyes and whirled around to face her greatest fear. Clay Miller. Right there. In the flesh. No longer safely confined to her memories and entwined with the song playing in her mind.

He stood there with the sun streaming in from the window behind him, outlining his tall muscular frame. His brown hair held not a touch of gray after all these years.

"Clay." Had she really said his name out loud? How many years had it been since she'd allowed herself to speak his name? Seventeen years. She knew the exact date.

Her breath froze in her lungs. Or did it burn? She

wasn't sure. Her eyes locked on his and she felt almost drunk with the sight of him. Her breath still wouldn't come. Nor any words. Her heart rammed against her rib cage and, for a moment, her emotions were so overwhelming she wasn't sure if she was going to burst into tears or crazy maniacal laughter.

He looked good. Older. His face had hardened at the edges. His eyes—those steel blue eyes that could either shine with laughter or freeze into cold, unfeeling hardness—stared back at her.

Clay looked over her shoulder at the jukebox, took a quick glance at the songs, and punched B19 without a moment's hesitation. "Our song."

Like it was normal to stand here talking to her. Like seventeen years hadn't passed in silence. Like she could deal with standing there, listening to their song.

He remembered too. Had he had any regrets? She doubted it. The pain of the breakup, so many years ago but still so fresh and raw when she thought of it, swept over her.

"Is it?" She lied, sure he didn't believe her. "I was just getting ready to play some current country songs." To prove her point, she dug into her purse for some more coins, dropped them in the jukebox, and hit a few more buttons.

She looked up at him, and his eyes told her he didn't believe her. Well, that wasn't her problem. He'd made it all too clear she wasn't his problem. So he wasn't hers either.

"You're looking good, Jenny."

His voice threw her again. Same voice, rolling over her as waves of memories crashed around her. She didn't answer him. Her voice wouldn't work, anyway. What did he want her to say? *Hey, it's great to see you?* Well, it wasn't.

He just stood there while the awkward silence thrust them apart. Good. That's what she needed. Distance.

Okay, he won. She'd talk. "You home visiting your mom?" She finally found her voice, though it sounded weak and tremulous.

"We're staying with her for a while. I'm working Doc Baker's clinic for him, while he takes a few weeks' vacation."

Once again her traitorous lungs refused to let in any oxygen. *Here? Our Doc Baker's clinic?* Now there was news she hadn't heard. How could she not know that? Why hadn't anyone told her? She knew why. Because the town had never forgotten. No one had wanted to be the one to tell her. It probably was the reason her friend, Becky Lee, had insisted Jenny come by the cafe today. Becky Lee needed to talk to her. Everyone would expect Becky Lee to break the news.

Becky Lee, bless her always-there-for-Jenny heart. She did know the secrets.

"Wh—what?" Jenny felt her life start to crumble around her. This was one thing she hadn't planned on.

Clay Miller, back in her life, even if it was only for a few weeks. She had always known there was a chance of seeing him when he came to visit his mother, Greta. Jenny had even seen him a few years ago, across the parking lot at the grocery store, trailed by two blonde girls. It had almost broken her heart at the time. Then a tall, gorgeous, blonde woman had gotten out of the car, dressed immaculately. It had been obvious, even from a distance, that the woman was ticked off at Clay. Jenny had heard snatches of the conversation drift across the parking lot.

"I'm sick of staying here." The blonde woman nagged at Clay. "You always drag us to this boring little town."

Clay had never even looked up to see Jenny standing there. She hadn't given him much of a chance, though. She had quickly ducked into her car, threw it in gear, and pulled out of the parking lot without going into the grocery store... without a backward glance.

Almost.

She hadn't been able to keep herself from one last look at him, walking into the store, with his youngest daughter clutching at his hand and dancing around at his side. The girl had tripped, and Clay had swiftly caught her before she had fallen. She had looked up at her father in adoration, with a look that said she was sure her daddy would never let her down.

That look had torn at her, making her unreasonably furious at fate. She'd sped the car out of the lot, away from the loving father and adoring daughter scene. She'd driven for hours that afternoon, down to the shore. She'd sat by the ocean and let her mind replay all her memories, torturing her, teasing her with "what ifs."

She had indulged in an entire afternoon of self-pity. Then she'd brushed off the sand, gotten into her car, and driven home to her son and her husband, resolutely putting Clay out of her mind once and for all.

When she had gotten home that night, her husband had known something was wrong, but then he had probably heard Clay was in town and figured it out. But he hadn't said a word. Joseph. He had always been there for her, too. Loved her. Protected her. Protected Nathan. She missed Joseph.

Her thoughts shot back to the present. Clay was still standing there. What was he saying?

"Can I get you some coffee?"

"No. Yes. Okay." *Had she said that? Had she actually agreed? Was she nuts?* Their song was just finishing. The haunting tones drifted into silence, replaced by the clanking of dishes and snatches of conversations at the busy cafe.

Clay led the way to a vinyl-covered booth at the back of the restaurant. Becky Lee pushed through the swinging door from the kitchen and stopped in her tracks. She looked at Jenny, an eyebrow raised and her bright red lipsticked mouth slightly open in surprise. She regained her composure and headed over to where Clay was sliding into the booth.

"As I live and breathe… If it isn't Clay Miller. I heard you were back in town. Your momma gonna give you a hand with those girls of yours? Bet she likes watching them too, now that she's retired from teaching. Though I heard she's been tutoring kids after school, and a handful this summer, too. So, you took over Doc Baker's practice for a bit. Good for you. Doc Baker needs a break. Can't remember the last time he took a vacation. I bet Greta is enjoying those girls of yours."

Jenny watched as Clay tried to take in all of Becky Lee's prattle. Full speed, Becky Lee rarely gave anyone a chance to answer. Clay had obviously forgotten that. He had actually opened his mouth to try and answer Becky Lee, but of course had no luck.

He flashed Jenny a grin. To her credit, she didn't react to his infectious grin. She didn't want to smile at him. Didn't want to be here, having coffee. Didn't want him to work at Doc Baker's. She didn't want him here in Comfort Crossing. She wasn't sure she even wanted him to be on the same planet.

Becky Lee continued right on. "Jenny, girl, you haven't been by in over a week."

"I know, I'm sorry. Been busy getting ready for the start of the new school year."

"So what do you kids want to order?"

"Couple of coffees." Clay looked at Jenny. "Black?"

Becky Lee shot Jenny a questioning look. They'd been

friends since grade school. Then Becky Lee had gone on to the public high school, while Jenny had been sent to the prestigious, private LeBlanc High School. But they had remained friends their whole lives.

Becky Lee, along with their friend Izzy Amaud, knew all about Clay, all about the past. Becky Lee and Izzy had kept her secret. They'd been there for her every step of the way. Becky Lee must think Jenny was certifiably nuts to be sitting here with the man who had caused her so much pain.

"Yes, black." Jenny nodded, hoping her cell phone would ring and she could make up an excuse to run. Or a hurricane would hit, or the roof fall in, or just anything in the world to get her out of there.

But Becky Lee didn't rescue her, she just shot her friend a quizzical look and left to retrieve the coffee. Some friend she was. Jenny fiddled with the saltshaker. The afternoon sun streamed in the window, shining on Clay, illuminating his watch and throwing arcs of reflections across the wall. She looked closely at the watch. *It couldn't be? Could it? The watch she had given him for high school graduation?* She stared at it.

Jenny was too shocked to say anything. The watch. After all these years. Why had he kept it? She couldn't believe the darn thing was still working.

"Mom told me about Joey. I'm sorry. You doing okay?"

Jenny pulled her glance away from the watch and

blinked at the sudden reference to her late husband. She'd almost forgotten Clay was the only one to ever get away with calling Joseph Joey. "I'm dealing with it."

"Your son? He's doing okay?" Clay continued.

"Nathan? He's doing as well as can be expected. He misses Joseph."

"Mom said Joey found out he had cancer, then was gone in a few months. Must have been hard on you."

The man had no idea how hard it had been. Her whole safe world had turned upside down. Nathan had taken it hard, acting out and getting into trouble. It was a good thing the sheriff had been friends with Joseph, he had brought Nathan home numerous times. Drinking. Fighting. He said that next time he'd have to take him in for underage drinking. She thanked him, but wondered if being sent off to jail for a night might knock some sense into Nathan. She sighed. It was hard on all of them.

But instead of explaining, she just said, "It's been difficult. Joseph's parents are taking it hard, too. At least they still have Nathan. They have always doted on him, but he seems to give them great comfort, now." She couldn't believe she was sitting here having this conversation with Clay.

Clay picked up the napkin bundled silverware and slowly unrolled it. He fiddled with the knife. "I should drop by and see them. Pay my respects."

"I'm sure they'd love to see you."

"I should have gone to see them before this. On one of

my trips in town. But… "

"I know. It was awkward."

"Awkward?" Clay's voice lowered. His eyes took on that hardened steel blue quality that could make a grown man take a step back. "I never thought you'd marry my best friend."

She braced herself against the blast of controlled anger emanating from Clay. What right did he have to judge her life? "You made it pretty clear you didn't want anything to do with me."

"Didn't take you long to start up a life with him, now, did it? You two had a son within a year. You moved on." His hands gripped the silverware he had unrolled.

Seventeen years of anger, resentment, and hurt rolled between them, threatening to suck them both down into its vortex. Jenny had had enough. She slowly slid to the end of the booth, the bare skin behind her knees sticking slightly to the vinyl seat. It took all her self-control to keep her voice down.

"You, Clay Miller, were the one who broke it off. You didn't want anything to do with me. You went off to college. You wanted to be free. Don't you dare say a word about what I did with my life after you dumped me."

"Jenns… I—"

She dug into her purse and dropped a few bills on the table for her yet to be delivered coffee. "I think it would be best if you just keep away from me. I'm glad you can help Doc Baker so he can take a vacation. He deserves it. But stay away from me. Keep your opinions about what I've done with my life to yourself. And don't you ever, *ever*, question my decision to marry Joseph. You lost that right the day you tossed me out of your life. The day you said you needed your freedom."

She left the cafe without saying what she really wanted to say to him. Yell at him. In the most childish immature manner. *This is all your fault, Clay Miller.*

* * * * *

Clay raked his hand through his hair. He'd mucked that one up, for sure. He watched Jenny stalk out the door, shoulders set, head high. He'd always admired the way she moved. Proud. Sure of herself. Her slight high school build had rounded. Her hair no longer hung loose on her shoulders like she had worn it in high school, but she had it pulled efficiently back in some kind of fancy braid thing. Darn, she looked good.

It had been a punch to his gut when he'd walked into the cafe today and had seen Jenny standing by the jukebox. Like the last seventeen years had just disappeared, and they were back in time when the world consisted of Jenny and Clay. Their future bright, their love declared proudly.

He smiled to himself. He hadn't believed her for one half second when she'd flippantly replied she didn't remember their song. She remembered. He could see it the depths of her honey-brown eyes. Remembrance

11

mixed with pain. The questions. Still. Seventeen years later. The ones he'd been avoiding all this time.

He watched her cross the street and slide into a gleaming red sports car. That's his Jenny Delacroix, always loved a fast car. *His Jenny?* What was he talking about? She hadn't been his for years. Not since she had come up to visit him, the second weekend of college, and he'd broken up with her. Besides, she wasn't even Jenny Delacroix anymore. She was Jenny Bouchard. His best friend's wife—no—widow. Ex-best friend, if that mattered anymore, since Joey was dead and they'd never be able to make their peace.

After all this time, his Jenny had never found out the truth. Clay pulled himself from his thoughts. Choices he had made. He couldn't change the past now.

Becky Lee came over with the coffee. "I see you managed to tick her off in less than five minutes."

Clay nodded his head. "Said something stupid. I should have kept my mouth shut."

"You're always doing something stupid when it comes to Jenny." Becky Lee never did pull any punches.

"Yep, isn't that the truth."

"She's had a rough year. She's struggling to regain her footing after Joseph's death. If you're going to mess with her mind again... well, just don't." She set down the coffee cups and nailed him with a no-nonsense look. "You broke Jenny's heart when you dumped her as soon as you were safe at Tulane med school with a full ride

12

from your impressive test scores. Married that Claire woman right away."

He didn't bother to correct her, that he'd married Claire after he found out Jenny had married Joey. Clay admired the way Becky Lee defended her friend. Becky Lee, Jenny, and Bella— Isabella, who Becky Lee and Jenny called Izzy—had always been each other's biggest fans. If only they knew the real reason he had broken up with Jenny, but there was no reason for the truth to come out now. "I know, Bec. She already warned me to stay away. I'm thinking that really is the best thing."

"Don't you go breaking her heart again, Clay Miller. She's come too far. She has enough on her hands with that son of hers."

"What's wrong with her son?" His mom hadn't told him anything was wrong with Jenny's son.

"Nothing's wrong with him. He's just an angry boy who lost his father. He's acting up in school, getting into minor problems with the cops. He's hurting and dealing with it in his own way. Jenny's afraid he's going to cross the line though, before he gets things all sorted out in his mind." Becky Lee refilled his coffee. "So, you just stay clear of her, Clay. I guess you'll head back home soon, anyway." She looked at him expectantly.

"Labor Day weekend. The girls' school starts later than the schools do here. Day after Labor Day."

"Good. You should be able to avoid each other for a few weeks." Becky walked away from the table.

Clay watched Becky Lee cross over to another table and cheerfully banter with the customers as she took their order. He wondered at life's twists. Here he was, having the same problem with his eldest daughter, Danielle, that Jenny was having with her son. Problems in school. Minor trouble with the cops. One of the reasons he had decided to come back to Comfort Crossing, Mississippi, for a few weeks. Danielle needed to get away from the crowd of kids she hung out with. He had to get her away from the kids who were dragging her into all kinds of messes.

Clay gulped down the coffee and tossed out a goodbye to Becky Lee. He had to stop by the clinic for a while. He was waiting for some test results on Mrs. Brown and he wanted to see who was on the schedule for tomorrow. Then he'd better go rescue Greta from her granddaughters. Lord knows, they could sure be a handful. But then, Greta always seemed to be able to deal with anything thrown her way and come out on top. Heck, at this point, she could probably handle the girls better than he could.

Becky Lee stopped him at the door, just as he grabbed the worn steel door handle and tried to make his escape into the sunshine and away from the memories.

"Clay?" Becky Lee snagged his elbow. Her eyes flashed with determination. "I mean it. Just leave Jenny alone."

Chapter Two

Clay tugged open the screen door to his mom's house. More than a house, it was a home. He loved that it was a few miles outside of town. It was just an old farmhouse, on the "wrong side of town," but it had been everything they had wanted or needed. His mom's house had three acres of land to roam, with a stream behind the property. It had been a great place to grow up.

The late afternoon sunshine flooded into the bright yellow kitchen as a gentle breeze ruffled the curtains at the window over the sink. It was a rare, cool summer's day. Greta had turned off the air conditioning and opened up the house to air it out. Tomorrow the temperature was supposed to climb back up to the nineties, a hot finish for the end of summer.

He could hear the bass tones thumping from the back of the house as soon as he entered the kitchen. Danielle must be locked in her room with the stereo blasting.

"Hey, Mom. How were the girls today?" He crossed over and pressed a quick kiss on his mother's cheek, reaching around her to swipe a carrot she was scraping.

"We were fine, son. I told you, we'll work things out."

"Want me to go tell Danielle to turn down the volume on her stereo?"

Greta laughed. "That *is* turned down. You should have heard it when she first slammed into her room."

"I'm sorry, Mom."

"It's all right. She was just angry I asked for help with the laundry. There were lots of long-suffering sighs and clattering around of the laundry baskets and hangers, but she helped."

"I told them both they were going to have to lend a hand around here. That you weren't going to be their live-in maid."

"Well, I actually got the feeling Danielle didn't mind helping, she just didn't want to let on that she didn't mind it."

Clay tried to swipe another carrot, but Greta swatted his hand away. "How's Abigail?"

"She's fine. They both came with me while I worked at the uniform exchange at the school. Danielle was appalled that kids actually had to wear uniforms to school."

"I bet she was." Clay smiled at the thought of his daughter wearing a uniform. At her school she wore the most outrageous outfits she could get away with. Midriff showing, bra straps hanging out of tank tops, low cut jeans. Way too low. The constant battles of sending her back to her room to change. He fondly remembered when the girls were little and he had just grabbed some cute little outfit his ex-wife had picked out for the girls, and pulled them into it. No arguments.

"Abigail, on the other hand, was intrigued with the whole idea of uniforms. She helped me sort out the sizes for the school uniform sale tomorrow."

"Thanks, Mom. I hope Danielle wasn't too much trouble."

Greta moved over to the stove and poked around in a few pots and stirred whatever wonderful smelling concoction she was making. He peeked over her shoulder. Gumbo. Clay's mouth instantly started watering. There was nothing quite like his mother's Cajun cooking.

Greta tossed a look over her shoulder to make sure Clay wasn't swiping more carrots. He was, of course, and she just rolled her eyes at him. "Danielle was fine, once she met some of the kids from high school who were hanging around. But you'll never believe who we saw."

"Who's that?" Clay asked the requisite question.

"Jenny Delacroix."

Jenny Bouchard, Clay silently corrected. Clay stopped crunching on the carrot. "Really?"

"She's helping at the sale tomorrow." Greta stirred the pot on the stove, releasing even more tantalizing scents into the kitchen. "Jenny picked up on Abigail's silence, and took it in stride. Abigail seemed to warm up to her right away. Jenny had her son, Nathan, with her. Danielle seemed to hit it off with him right away, too."

"I hear he's getting into trouble with the cops. He needs to stay away from Danielle."

"Like Danielle isn't getting into trouble? They are just two kids who have had a rough few years and are trying to catch their footing." Greta ended that discussion with a no nonsense decision and a resounding clatter of the lid dropping back on top of the pot.

"Anyway, like I said, Danielle and Nathan hit it off. He's a good kid, just a little overwhelmed with life right now." Greta swiped a curl away from her face. "Hand me the salt, would you, please?"

Clay reached over, grabbed the saltshaker, and passed it over to Greta. He shook his head. Here he was, promising himself he'd keep his distance, and Jenny's son was befriending his daughter. Well, they'd probably never see each other again anyway. He turned as he heard Abigail enter the kitchen. She came over and smiled at him and gave him a quick hug.

"How's your day, pumpkin?"

His daughter smiled at him and spun around showing off a new dress she was wearing.

"Looks good."

"I took the girls shopping today. It's not often I get the chance to spoil them." Greta smiled at her granddaughter.

Abigail ran her hands down the fabric of the skirt and pushed it precisely back in place. She nodded at her father. Her brilliant blue eyes sparkled up at him. What he wouldn't give to make everything in her life all better again.

"Oh and my car is acting up again, so I dropped it at the garage and Ernie gave us a ride home. If you can take us into town tomorrow, Ernie said he'd run the car over to the school for me after he got it fixed."

"Mom, you need a new car." The car was twelve years old and he wished she'd buy a newer one. It was always in the repair shop for one thing or the other. He was afraid it would leave her stranded.

"I like my car." Greta dismissed the idea of replacing the car as quickly as she'd dismissed the idea of replacing the worn kitchen table or the faded sofa in the front room. They were still serviceable. No need for change.

"Abby, sweetie, why don't you run upstairs and tell Danielle it's five minutes until dinner time."

Abigail nodded to her grandmother and disappeared from the room. Clay heard her steps on the wooden stairway. The music got momentarily louder as Danielle's door opened, and he heard hushed voices as Danielle spoke to her sister. Danielle was so good with Abigail, a blatant contrast to her dislike of just about everything else about her world these days.

Clay sighed. What he wouldn't give to hear his

younger daughter's voice instead of her constant nodding. Abigail hadn't said a word since her mother left. None of the doctors and specialists he'd taken her to could help. They all said to give it time. Here he was, a doctor himself, and he couldn't seem to help either daughter. One was out of control, and one wouldn't speak. Some father he was.

"It will be okay, son. You'll see. You'll work things out. You just need to give them both some time."

Clay crossed over and gave his mom a quick hug. She'd always been able to read his mind. She called it her "mother connection." Mustn't be a universal mother thing though, because his ex-wife sure hadn't been able to connect to their daughters—a true, if harsh, reality.

He walked over to the cabinets and pulled open the doors. Some things don't change. The dinner plates and glasses had been in this cabinet his whole life. He needed that now, the steady comfort of knowing where things were. Predictability. From the simple white stoneware dishes to the chrome and Formica table, still the same after all these years. He grabbed the plates and started to set the table.

"Oh, and Clay?" Greta paused, spoon poised over the pot as she dished up supper. "Nathan asked if we were going to the Festival Days, this weekend. I said yes and we'd meet them there."

In spite of his best intentions, the dinner plate he was holding slipped from his hands, crashed to the floor, and shattered into hundreds of tiny shards.

* * * * *

Jenny, Becky Lee, and Izzy sat in the sunroom of Izzy's new home. Izzy and her two boys had moved into the converted carriage house, on the same property as her store, Bella's Vintage Shop, at the beginning of the summer.

"How are things going with the store since the move?" Becky Lee took a sip of sweet tea and put her feet up on the ottoman.

"I'm kind of surprised. I'm getting almost the same traffic through the store here on Rosewood Avenue as I did when it was on Main Street. I love all the window light and different rooms to set up my displays. It's such a cute Victorian house, too," Izzy said.

"I'm glad it all worked out." Jenny leaned back on the sofa, drained from the emotional turmoil of seeing Clay again. "How are things going with the renovations on your old shop? Is Sylvia going to open her restaurant soon?"

"They're going great. Sylvia is hoping to reopen her restaurant by Labor Day weekend. Owen did a great thing buying the building and giving it to Sylvia. Even if it did mean I had to move my shop."

Izzy had leased the space on Main Street for her shop and lived over the shop with her two boys, but when Owen bought the building, she had lost both her shop space and her home. Unfortunately, Owen and Izzy had fallen for each other, but then Izzy found out Owen was the one responsible for her losing her shop and home. Things had gotten worse when Izzy's ex-husband had threatened to take custody of the boys, since she no longer had an income coming in from the shop, or a place to live.

Owen had eventually worked out a deal that benefited both he and Izzy, where she could rent this new space on Rosewood Avenue for her shop and to live. He had been renovating the old space and had given it to his half-brother, Jake. Jake and his mother, Sylvia, were going to open a restaurant in the building. The building had been in their family for generations, until they were forced to sell it to pay Sylvia's medical bills. Owen had been happy to buy the building and give it back to them. Once Izzy found out Owen had bought the building because he believed it was owed to Jake and Sylvia, she was not only no longer angry with Owen, but she had respected his decision. Izzy and Owen had started dating again and Jenny was glad to see her friend so happy. Things looked to be getting serious between the couple.

Izzy interrupted Jenny's thoughts. "I hear Clay is back in town and you ran into him at Magnolia Cafe. You okay?"

"I'm fine. It was just a shock, seeing him standing there like that. Then, for some unknown reason, I said yes to having coffee with him. I never learn."

"Not that she ever got to drink her coffee. It only took a

few minutes for Clay to make our Jenny girl mad." Becky Lee chimed in.

"I told him to just stay away from me while he's in town."

"You sure that's what you really want?" Izzy asked.

Jenny sighed. "I don't know what I want, but I know I don't trust him. I know I'm furious with myself for my reaction when I first saw him again. You'd think I'd get over that whole heart flip-flop thing when I see him. It's been years. He tore my life apart. And yet, my traitorous heart just won't listen to me."

Becky Lee leaned over and put her hand on Jenny's knee. "You know, Clay being in town might give you an opportunity—"

"Don't say it, Bec. It's nothing I haven't thought of myself." Jenny looked at her friends, the ones who had kept her secret for so many years. This probably was a good opportunity, but she wasn't ready to take that first step. She was a coward and it didn't make her feel good about herself. Not one bit.

She sighed. She really did need to see Clay once more. It was time.

Chapter Three

The next morning, Jenny called up the stairs. "Nathan, hurry up. We're going to be late." She could hear her son clomping around upstairs. He'd slept through three swats at his snooze alarm before she had gone in and pulled the covers off him and told him to get moving. Now he was still getting ready, hadn't had breakfast, and she had wanted to get to school early today. She needed to start setting up her classroom for the new school year that started the following week, and she'd promised to work at the uniform sale that afternoon. Nathan was headed to help his grandfather at his law firm for the morning. He often helped out there, filing and doing miscellaneous office chores. The two seemed to enjoy the time together.

Joseph had been a lawyer in the firm, too. Jenny had always figured that the three of them would be in the practice together, someday. Bouchard, Bouchard, and

Bouchard. It wouldn't be happening now, but Joseph's father seemed to be grooming Nathan for a career in the legal field, if Nathan didn't end up with a felony on his record first. Jenny sighed.

"Nathan, I mean it. We're leaving right now."

Her son clattered down the stairs and appeared in the kitchen. "I'm ready."

It still startled her, sometimes, how tall he'd become, this man child standing before her. She wasn't sure when the transformation had happened. In her mind he was just about kindergarten age. But here, in the flesh, was a young man who shaved irregularly and was a head taller than she was. She had always imagined the scene at the bathroom sink, where Joseph stood beside Nathan and showed him how to shave. But that hadn't happened. Joseph had died before Nathan had even grown a hint of a beard. She wasn't sure how Nathan learned to shave. She'd bought him an electric razor, but noticed he used a real razor and shaving cream instead. The fresh scent of his after-shave wafted through the kitchen as he breezed through.

He was dressed in khakis and a blue collared shirt. He had shaved this morning, and looked impossibly clean cut, which always seemed to surprise people, when he'd gotten into so much trouble this last year. Here before her stood the all-American, clean-cut, high school boy. Probably made it easier for him to get away with his shenanigans.

Nathan grabbed an apple from the table and pushed out the door. Whatever happened to family breakfast, and laughter, and an extra cup of coffee? Gone were those days. Once Joseph had died, the sit down meals had disappeared. It was so painful to sit at the wooden kitchen table and stare at the empty chair that had been Joseph's for all these years.

She resolved to change things this school year. Try to pull off a few more family dinners. Actually sit down to breakfast with Nathan.

She crossed the driveway and climbed into the passenger seat of the car. Nathan, the driver, always wanted to be the one behind the wheel ever since he got his license a few months ago. He threw the car into reverse and pulled out of the driveway, apologizing insincerely when the tires squealed on the already warm pavement.

* * * * *

"Danielle! Let's go." Clay turned to smile at Abigail, who had been ready for at least thirty minutes, sitting at the kitchen table, swinging her leg back and forth. "Danielle, your grandmother needs to go. We're all leaving."

Greta stacked the breakfasted dishes and they clattered into the sink. "She needs to eat breakfast."

"I know, Mom. It's a battle I lost years ago. Danielle doesn't eat breakfast. I try and pick my battles these days."

Clay grabbed his medical bag, cell phone, and car

keys. "I mean it. We're leaving, Danielle." He planned to drop his mother and the girls off at the school on his way to work.

His daughter flounced into the kitchen, her shirt exposing inches of uncovered stomach above the low waistband of her very short jean skirt. "I can't believe I have to get up this early."

Clay took one look at her outfit and said, "Go up and change. Grams won't want you looking like that at school while she's working."

Danielle shot him a look that clearly said he was out of his mind. "I don't want to look like a dork. A lot of the kids from high school will be there today."

"Clay, it's okay. She looks fine," Greta said.

"See, Grams doesn't want me to look dorky."

Clay decided that didn't even warrant a reply. Actually, his daughter looked beautiful, as always, her blonde hair brushed and shiny in the morning light filtering in the window. She had flawless skin with a healthy glow on her cheeks, though how she had a healthy glow was beyond him, because getting her to eat a healthy diet and exercise was a constant battle of frustration and clash of wills. A two-year-old's temperament in a sixteen-year-old's body. With a lot of skin showing.

"Okay, we're leaving." Greta swooshed them all out the door, not bothering to lock it behind her. "Come on, we're going to have a great time."

Danielle didn't look convinced. Clay shot her a cut-it-out stare. So far, he didn't have a very good feeling about today.

As the morning progressed, he realized his expectations of the day were probably more realistic than his mother's. First, there was an accident on the bridge over the railroad tracks, going over to the east side of Comfort Crossing. It had always appealed to his wry sense of humor, that he did indeed live on the wrong side of the tracks.

He drove them into town and down the brick cobblestones of Main Street. He loved that Comfort Crossing still had a bustling downtown area and hadn't died a slow death, like so many small towns had, in the last ten or twenty years. They drove past the city park on Main Street and turned down Elm Street to reach LeBlanc School. By the time he got them there, his beeper had already gone off twice. He had to use the old fashioned technology of a pager in Comfort Crossing, with its patchy cell phone service. He needed to get to the clinic, pronto. Clay maneuvered the car up to the front of the school and Danielle slid out of the car. Her skirt barely covered her rear end. She was going to be the death of him.

Greta got out and held out her hand to Abigail. Clay glanced at his wristwatch. Really late now.

He watched as a good-looking kid came up to the car. "Hey, Danielle."

"Hey, Nathan."

The boy poked his head into the open passenger side window and held out his hand. "Hello, sir. I'm Nathan Bouchard."

It hit Clay in his gut. The boy had his mother's curly brown hair and a faint dimple on his left check as he smiled, just like his mom. Clay searched the boy's face for signs of his best friend, Joey, but he could only see his mother's impact on him. Except for his eyes. For the life of him, Clay couldn't remember what color Joey's eyes were, but they must have been blue. Nathan had remarkably clear blue eyes.

"Clay Miller. Nice to meet you, too." Clay shook the boy's outstretched hand. Good strong grip. Good manners. It was hard to imagine this was the same boy Becky Lee said was giving his mother so much trouble.

"Come on, Danielle, I'll show you around and introduce you to some kids before I have to go work at my grandfather's. That's okay, Mrs. Miller?" Nathan asked Greta.

"Sure. Just check in with me every so often, okay? And, Danielle, don't leave the school."

"Thanks, Grams." Danielle looked at Clay as if she expected him to object. Clay just nodded his okay. The boy turned and led Danielle away into the school.

Clay watched them head in the front door. How many times had he climbed those same stairs? Always feeling just a little left out, no matter what he did. He shook away the memories.

"Mom, call me if your car isn't ready and you need to be picked up."

"Will do."

Greta and Abigail headed into the school. To make matters worse, Clay spotted Jenny walking into the school at the same time. She paused and spoke with Greta, then bent down and said something to Abigail. He watched as Abigail smiled, then slipped her hand into Jenny's.

* * * * *

Velda, the woman who ran the front desk at Dr. Baker's office, greeted him with a litany of problems the moment he walked in the door. "Your first patient cancelled, but there's already a waiting room full of people. Susie Jennings' youngest looks like he might need a few stitches. And Mrs. Valley is sure she's going into labor. Again. She's been saying that every other day for three weeks, now."

Velda, trained as a nurse and all around right hand man—woman—was going to be his saving grace. Bless her for being there while Doc Baker was gone. Clay was going to have to get used to this family practice gig. He'd been in a busy practice in the city, but had never really had much time to get to know his patients. Being on call once every five weeks was nothing like the twenty-four seven thing he had going now. He had actually enjoyed getting to know these patients a bit in the few days he'd been here. He'd even gone to school with a few of them, and they were quick to fill him in on the happenings around town.

He walked up to the counter. "Okay, hit me, Velda."

She dumped a stack of charts in his hands and turned toward the waiting room. "Mrs. Valley, Dr. Miller will see you now."

By late afternoon he had cleared out the patients and Velda had given him the message that he needed to pick up Greta and the girls because Greta's car hadn't been fixed.

"I guess I'm out of here, Velda."

"I'll lock everything up," Velda said in her life-saving, efficient manner. "See you tomorrow."

"Thanks for everything. You're the only reason I made it through today."

"Just so I'm appreciated." The woman flashed him a smile. "Run along now." She pushed him out the door.

He drove to the school and parked in the side parking lot. He didn't want to go inside, but it looked like he had no choice. The past hit him like the same fleeting wave of nausea that had punched him the first time he'd carved into a cadaver.

He pushed the door and reluctantly entered. The past was right there, the same not-quite-fitting-in feeling chasing his senses. The feeling of injustice, when his scholarship had been pulled in the last year of school and he'd had to quit the football team, work two jobs, and Greta had to take on extra students to tutor to make enough for him to finish school there. He knew who was behind the scholarship withdrawal. Everyone did, but no one admitted it. Jenny's father. Old Man Delacroix had shown his extreme displeasure that Clay had dared to date his daughter by seeing the scholarship was pulled.

Clay took a deep breath and resolutely headed to the gymnasium where they held the uniform sales. Abigail came skipping up to him as soon as he walked through the door. Greta was boxing up the last of the uniforms and Danielle was hanging out on the bleachers with some other kids. He noticed that Nathan was close by her side.

Then he saw her.

Jenny.

She still had the ability to take his breath away. He didn't like it one bit. He was a grown man, not a high school kid with a crush. He should be over it by now. Way over it. He watched her talking to some parents and laughing. She reached her hand up and brushed her hair back from her face, a movement he remembered so vividly from the past.

She turned and he knew the exact moment she spotted him. For a moment she flashed him a big smile, but it was as though she realized the time and place, and the smile faded slowly into the past.

Danielle and Nathan wound their way over to where

he was standing. What was Danielle saying? He pulled his gaze away from Jenny.

"Dad, are you listening to me?" Danielle was obviously repeating herself.

He tried to pull the confused parent look off his face long enough to focus.

With a look that said she had noticed his half attention to what she was saying, and eager to press her advantage, Danielle forged on. "Some kids are headed over to a place called Magnolia Cafe. Can I go?"

Clay just stood and was sure he looked bewildered. Jenny had that effect on him. He watched as she crossed the gym towards them. "No, I have to get back to the office, write up some charts and make some phone calls after I drive you all home."

"I could drive her home afterwards, couldn't I, Mom?" Nathan joined in on the ambush as Jenny walked up to them.

"That's fine with me, but you'll have to ask Dr. Miller."

"Sir?"

Clay looked cornered. "Well, I don't know."

Jenny stepped in as only a mother, who had quickly assessed the situation, could. She seemed to realize Clay didn't know Nathan at all and wasn't comfortable letting his daughter ride with a stranger. Just good parenting, Clay assured himself.

"How about we all head there for a bit? I could use a big ice cream sundae after my day. How about it? Do you have time?"

Jenny questioned Clay. She'd given him an out. He wouldn't have to leave his daughter in the hands of some unknown teenager, but darned if Jenny didn't look like she expected him to turn her down.

Abigail tugged on her father's hand, a questioning look in her eyes. Clay scrubbed his hand through his hair, torn in his decision.

"Okay. For just a bit. That work for you, Danielle?" His daughter was obviously not very pleased to find her dad was going too, but she was smart enough to realize this was the closest she was going to get to a yes.

Clay turned to his mom. "Okay with you if we go for ice cream on the way home?"

"Fine by me."

Greta stared strangely at Nathan. Then at Clay. Then at Jenny. *What was up with that?* He shoved the thought aside. Being around Jenny jangled his thoughts.

* * * * *

Jenny couldn't believe she had offered this option. Once again she'd be spending time with Clay. She must be nuts. But she couldn't seem to help herself. This man she had hated and despised for walking out on her. This man, who, when she was being really honest, still held a spell over her and always would, no matter how much she denied it. No matter how much she didn't want it to be so. The fact was, Clay Miller could still take her breath away with his smile, which spread all the way to his twinkling blue eyes.

Jenny knew she was stalling as she lagged behind the others. She'd already said she would go. What made her suggest this? She'd promised herself she would avoid Clay for the few weeks he was in town. Except for one time. She had to have a serious conversation with him. It was time he knew the truth. No more excuses. She wasn't a scared high school girl anymore. He had a right to know, she knew that. But once she told him the truth, she wouldn't have to worry about seeing him, because he'd quite possibly never speak to her again.

She caught up with them as they were walking out the door. The blast of humid air sucked her breath away for a moment and shimmers of heat danced across the parking lot. Danielle and Nathan walked in step with Clay, while Abigail trailed closely behind, her hand in Greta's. They all turned and waited for her on the front steps of the school as she pushed through the doors and into the sunlight.

The sight took her breath away. There was her Nathan, standing tall and proud next to Clay, both of them oblivious to any resemblance. Neither of them aware that they were father and son.

Chapter Four

Becky Lee looked up as they slipped into the cafe. She flashed a disbelieving look at Jenny, who only shrugged in return, and then looked at Nathan. Then looked at Clay. Back to Nathan. She shook her head and motioned for them to come in. The place was packed, with kids hanging out at the counter and in the back booths. Becky Lee crossed over to where they stood.

"Becky Lee, these are Clay's girls, Danielle and Abigail."

"Hey, girls. Good to meet you."

"Nice to meet you," Danielle answered.

"Hey, Miss Bec." Nathan greeted her.

Jenny was suddenly reminded of when he was a toddler. When she'd point to someone and Nathan would say their name, and then clap his chubby little hands. It had been too cute. Her very next thought was how Clay had missed that. He'd missed everything.

Becky Lee broke into her thoughts. "Why don't you kids head over to the counter? Abigail, do you want one of my special ice cream sodas?"

Abigail flashed a big smile and nodded enthusiastically. Greta saw a friend at the counter and went off to chat with her.

Nathan grabbed Danielle's elbow. "Come on, back here."

"Wait." She pulled away briefly. "Come on, Abby, you come back with us." She turned to Nathan. "That's okay, right?" Her tone said there would be no argument.

It didn't appear Nathan wanted to argue about it anyway. "Sure. Come on, Short Stuff. You come hang with us." Abigail looked up at the boy with wide adoring eyes. It appeared Abigail had found a new hero.

The truth crept up her spine, sending a shiver through her. A hero in the brother she didn't even know she had. Nathan led his sisters—*sisters*—over to the counter and they were greeted by a bunch of his friends. *Bury the thought for now.*

Jenny shook her head. She couldn't figure out how her son could be such a good, kind-hearted kid one moment, and have her tearing her hair out the next. She turned her attention to Becky Lee, who was weaving her way through the crowd. Her friend motioned to one of the last empty booths, away from the crowd of teenagers.

Jenny and Clay wound their way through to the far end of the cafe and slid into the seats. The air conditioner hummed away, trying vainly to cool off the place after the surge of warm bodied teens had descended. Not much had changed over the years. This had been where Clay and Jenny had come after school, all those years ago.

"I didn't know if I should intervene or not."

Clay looked up at her, a question in his blue eyes.

"I could see you didn't want Danielle to go off with Nathan. I know you don't know him. But I figured you'd want her to come and make friends. I thought this might be a compromise. I didn't mean to interfere with your parenting."

"No, it was a good idea. Doubt if I would have thought of it." A slow smile crept across Clay's face. "Besides, I could do with an ice cream sundae myself."

Becky Lee made it over to their table, menus tucked under her arm, and an order pad clutched in her hand. "Hey, kiddos. What can I do you for? The usual, Jenny?"

"Double the chocolate, please."

"Wow, that bad?" Becky Lee grinned at her.

Her friend knew her too well. "That bad."

"Okay one ice cream sundae, double the chocolate, coming up."

"Clay?" She pinned him with a you'd-better-be-good look.

"I'll have the same."

"Okay, two of 'em. Coming up."

Jenny did not miss the look of incredulity Becky Lee

threw in her direction. No kidding. She thought this whole situation was a little out of control herself. So much for her pronouncement that Clay should stay away from her.

* * * * *

Clay looked over to the counter, watching Becky Lee take Abigail behind the counter to help make the sundaes. Abby's face held a fierce concentration as she slowly scooped the ice cream into the glasses. Becky Lee was great with her, patiently letting his daughter take her time. He turned back to Jenny.

He was still slightly stunned to be sitting here with her, just like they had done years and years ago. A different time and place. A lifetime ago. Yet, it seemed so right. Like no time had passed.

But it had. He knew that. They both had responsibilities and children to raise. She had married his best friend. She still believed he hadn't wanted her all those years ago, that he had really wanted the wild and carefree college boy life. He wasn't about to bring up the truth now, after all these years. What good would it do? Besides, Greta had told him Jenny's father was very sick, and wasn't expected to make it through the year. She didn't need to know this now. She had enough to deal with. Her husband had died and her father was dying. Old Man Delacroix might be a heartless jerk, but he was still Jenny's father.

To be honest, though, now that he had a daughter in

high school, he wasn't sure what lengths he'd go to keep her away from some boy he thought wasn't good for her. Though he hoped he wouldn't base his opinion on where the boy lived or how much his family had, which was basically what Jenny's father had hated about him. He was from the wrong side of the tracks.

Clay dragged his thoughts from the past he couldn't change, to the future he had some control over. He looked across the restaurant to where Danielle was sitting on a stool by the counter. Abigail was perched on the next stool, and Nathan was on her other side. Protected and included. He often marveled at how well the two girls got along, his rebel daughter, Danielle, who took such good care of her little sister. One of the few things he could depend on.

"Danielle seems very protective of Abigail."

Clay turned and stared at Jenny. His heartbeat quickened, with an almost imperceptible change in rhythm. They used to have that connection all the time, where they could almost read each other's thoughts. It had been years. Could it possibly still be there after all this time?

Jenny sat there, looking at him, unaware of what her simple question had done to him. Torn him up. Reminded him of what they had lost—what *he* had lost. What his decision to break up with her had cost him.

He had even gone to see Joey about a year after he had broken up with Jenny. He wasn't sure why, but he had told Joey the reason he had broken up with Jenny. But it had been too late. Joey and Jenny had Nathan by then, so he had married Claire. Clay had seen the look of sympathy in Joey's eyes, he knew Joey could feel his pain. But there had been something else lingering in Joey's look he hadn't been able to figure out. Joey had yelled at him for letting Jenny's old man coerce him into making a stupid decision. One that had cost him Jenny. Nothing Clay could do would change what had happened. Joey had told him to go away and not come back, not to hurt Jenny by dragging up the past. That had been the last time he'd ever talked to Joey.

"She's good with Abigail."

"What?" Jenny's voice pulled him back from his thoughts.

"Danielle. Not a lot of older sisters would put up with dragging their little sister along to the local hangout."

"Not a lot of boys would have been okay with it either." Clay complimented Nathan's easy acceptance of Abigail's presence.

"Well, Nathan is unpredictable, to say the least." Jenny looked over at the kids. "So Abigail doesn't talk?"

"Not a word since her mother moved out. Not a sound."

"That's rough."

"It is. The girls are having quite a few adjustment problems." He could see the empathy in Jenny's eyes. "Bec mentioned you were having some problems with

Nathan?" Clay wasn't sure if this was a safe subject to bring up or not.

Jenny twisted the rolled up silverware. "He's a good kid. He is. He's just having a really hard time dealing with losing Joseph. I think he's pulling out of it, though. We haven't had any, um… *incidents*… in a little while now."

"It's hard on a kid to lose a parent. Danielle is dealing with her mother moving out of the house by acting up. Breaking rules. Nothing big, just rebelling at the fates, I guess. Making some poor choices."

Jenny flashed him a sad smile. "That's exactly how it is with Nathan, rebelling at the fates. That's a really good way to put it."

He knew Jenny was too polite to ask him the question on her mind. He could see it in her eyes. *Why did your wife move out?* He wasn't sure he was ready to discuss that with Jenny. He hadn't come to grips with it himself. Why his wife—why did he still call her that—why his ex-wife moved out. Left him. But what boggled his mind even more than her deserting him, was the fact Claire could leave her daughters behind.

Becky Lee saved him from any other deep thoughts, or attempts at explaining his screwed up life, by depositing their ice cream sundaes in front of them. "Good looking kids you two have." She nodded towards the three kids at the counter.

* * * * *

Jenny stared at the three kids sitting side by side, all three of Clay's offspring. The thought rocked her to her core. It grabbed her hard in the gut. She watched them sitting there, full of laughter. She was suddenly afraid that anyone looking at Nathan and Clay would instantly figure it out.

Once again she was wracked with guilt over her decision to keep Nathan's real father's identity a secret. Many times she had felt Clay—and Nathan—deserved to know the truth, but then she thought of all Joseph had done for them. All his parents had done for them, and how close Joseph's parents still were to Nathan. What would they do if they found out the truth? They had lost their only son. She'd be taking away their only grandchild, too.

Besides, Jenny had never wanted Clay to marry her because of some twisted sense of duty. Nathan deserved better than that. *She* deserved better than that. Joseph had wanted the two of them, right off the bat. She'd told Joseph the truth—that she was carrying Clay's child—but he had still asked her to marry him. Nathan had deserved a father who wanted him, no questions asked. He had gotten that with Joseph.

Jenny had felt guilty her whole life over the decision she had made and the secrets she had kept. But, looking back, she didn't think she'd do anything differently. Nathan had had a wonderful life. He'd adored Joseph. Joseph had been the ultimate in a great father from helping with schoolwork, to teaching him to throw a baseball, to just hanging out with his son and talking to him. The man had truly loved Nathan as his own.

Now, things were different. Before he had died, Joseph had made Jenny promise she would tell Clay and Nathan the truth. Now Clay was in town and she was out of excuses. But Jenny still had to put Nathan first, and do what was best for him. She wasn't sure he could deal with another shock right now. He was having a hard enough time dealing with losing Joseph. If he found out the truth, he'd have to deal with losing Joseph all over again. Not to mention she couldn't bear to hurt Joseph's parents either.

But, in that one moment, seeing all of Clay's children sitting together, she knew what she had to do. She knew the time was right, even if it turned everyone's lives upside down. Clay deserved the truth. She deliberately pulled her stare away from the kids and back to Clay. She'd tell him this week, but not with everyone around. She'd tell him when they were alone.

This week, she promised herself. First, she was going to get to know the new Clay, this older Clay sitting before her with his steel blue eyes and warm, infectious smile. But she was going to ignore these things she remembered so well about him. She was.

"So, are your girls having a good time with Greta?"

"I think so. And Mom likes having the girls there, I know that. Though I'm not sure how much she likes Danielle's stereo and music choices."

"So, I guess your girls are having a hard time dealing with the loss of their mother, too?"

"Loss is a nice way to put it. She left us. Me. Them. She's seen them like two times in the last six months." Clay fiddled with his watch and turned to look at the girls sitting at the counter.

"I'm sorry, Clay." She looked at his face, edged with pain.

"It was a mess. Abigail hasn't said another word since I sat the girls down and told them their mother was moving out. Claire, my wife, no—my ex-wife—didn't even have the decency to tell the girls she was leaving, left it up to me. Danielle spent the better part of a month in her room, then came out this changed creature. Rebellious. Apathetic about her schoolwork. Dropped out of sports. The only thing that remained the same was her attitude toward Abigail." Clay slowly pushed the long handled spoon into the ice cream sundae and shovelled out a big mouthful. "Danielle seems to blame me. She heard her mother and I having an argument right before her mother left. I'm sure she thinks if we hadn't argued, her mother would still be with her."

"You can't blame yourself. Married people argue. One argument doesn't cause a woman to leave."

"No, but I often wonder. If only I hadn't argued with her that day. Did it push her over the line?"

"If onlys. They really get to you sometimes, don't they?" She should know. She was an expert in the if-only game.

He dug another huge spoonful of ice cream from the fountain glass. "I guess I'll always wonder. The choices we make... The outcome from them."

She could see the tiredness at the corners of his eyes. There was no mistaking the blame he was putting on himself. "You're still doing a good job raising those girls. Abigail will come around soon. She probably just needs time."

"I hope so. There's been a lot of changes in her life in the last year. Her mom leaving. Claire breezes in occasionally and takes them shopping or out to dinner. Then she disappears for months. Never goes to the girls' school things. Never goes to their sports... not that Danielle plays any sports anymore. I'm working a lot more hours because..." Clay paused and looked at her, seemingly unsure if he should go on. "Because I need to."

He obviously wasn't going to explain further. Jenny started to reach out and touch his hand, but caught herself just in time. "If anyone can make a child feel safe and secure, it's Greta. I remember when we were kids, how she always made time for me, always listened to me. She taught me how to bake pies, remember that? My mom had always had cooks who did all the baking and cooking. But I so wanted to learn how to make your favorite apple pie. We made four pies, that afternoon when she taught me. Until we both agreed I'd made as fine a pie as she had. Well, almost."

47

Clay flashed a slow lazy grin. "I remember that. I came home and the kitchen was covered with flour... and so were you. I ate pie for days. Remember, Joey was with me and he said he hated apple pie, but you made him have a piece anyway?"

Jenny dug into her sundae. The memories were all flooding back now. The ache of the loss of Joseph tugged at her. At odd moments it crept up and overcame her. She and Joseph had loved each other as friends, though maybe that had changed for Joseph as the years went by. It seemed to have grown into something more for him, though he never talked about it. He'd been so good to her and Nathan. He'd deserved so much better than she'd given him, but she had cared deeply for him. She had loved him, in her own way. A way that was different than how she had loved Clay.

The silence drifted across the table, separating them. Waves of memories and regrets washed over her.

"So, I never knew Joseph had a thing for you." Clay broke the silence into tiny brittle pieces.

"He—He didn't. I mean..." What was she supposed to say? Joseph had cared about her. He'd just started out wanting to be her white knight, to rescue her from her unwed motherhood. They hadn't meant for it to be permanent. Just give the child a name and a father. But somehow, it had just grown. Joseph had been decidedly nuts about Nathan, from the first moment he held the baby in his arms. Their life had just blossomed from there.

"I mean, you got married within weeks of us breaking up." His eyes held a trace of bitterness, possibly a hint of anger.

"*We* didn't break up. *You* broke up with me. Wanted all that college freedom. Done with the high school crush. No questions asked. Nothing I said could change your mind. So don't go saying ridiculous stuff like when *we* broke up." Jenny gritted her teeth against the other words she wanted to throw at him. How he'd left her all alone to deal with a baby.

"It probably worked out for the best, anyway." He punched his words at her. "You were raised with everything. Money. Power. Generations of Comfort Crossing upper class. I was the boy from the wrong side of the tracks."

"I never felt that way." She started to reach across the table, to touch his clenched hand, the knuckles white from the pressure. She caught herself and placed her hand in her lap. Far away from Clay.

"You would have." Clay insisted.

"You don't give me much credit, Clay Miller. And if you really thought that was how I felt, then you didn't really know me after all." Her heart pounded in her chest. Riotous emotions careened through her. She felt betrayed all over again, that he could have thought her that shallow.

"Maybe I didn't know you." Clay dropped the spoon

on the table. "Maybe I didn't know myself."

* * * * *

Clay suddenly decided the sundae held no appeal. Jenny sat across from him, with a look of hurt so deeply embedded in her eyes that it tore at him to his very being. He'd put that look there. Again. He was always hurting Jenny. It seemed like all she ever knew from him was pain.

He slid his hand over his face, feeling the late afternoon whiskers scratch at his palm. This was getting them nowhere. Here he was acting like a jerk about Jenny marrying Joey. And why shouldn't she have? He had dropped her. Bang. No discussion.

He wadded up his napkin and tossed it on the table, noticing Jenny wasn't touching her sundae either.

Laughter suddenly erupted from across the room. Clay twisted to see what was going on and knocked over his sundae as he abruptly stood up.

Nathan was talking to Abigail, and she was laughing. She was laughing *out loud*.

Clay strode across the distance. When he got closer, he saw tears threatening the corners of Danielle's eyes, and she flashed him a "stay back" sign behind Abigail's back.

There it was again. His beautiful baby girl's laughter. The sound of it washed over his heart, making him believe there was hope for the future. That maybe Greta was right and things would work out.

He looked over Abigail's head at his oldest daughter, who was now trying valiantly to fight back the tears. Well, he'd give her credit. He felt like crying himself. His wonderful, gorgeous, adorable child was laughing. Out loud. *Did everyone hear that? Like a fine-tuned engine, purring to life. Was that not the most beautiful sound in the world?*

He felt Jenny come up beside him and place her hand on his arm. He looked down at her and the instant connection jolted through him. She knew what he was feeling. He could feel her connecting to his emotions.

"Leave them be, for a bit." Jenny's voice was low.

He turned and led the way back to the table. "I'll be forever in your son's debt."

Jenny just smiled as she slipped back into the booth. The late afternoon sun shone on the cinnamon highlights in her hair. She reached across and placed her hand over his, giving him her Jenny smile. That warm smile that made him feel like he was the only person in the room, the only person in her universe. He had missed that smile.

Chapter Five

Jenny hurried home from school. She had spent the day preparing her classroom for the upcoming school year and needed to go home, change, and get back to school for the big end of the summer Festival Days Picnic. She'd picked up fried chicken and made some potato salad and brownies. Festival Days had been a tradition since she had been a little girl. Everyone came – the students, their parents, grandparents, teachers and staff. The cheerleaders cheered and the football players paraded around the field. The school band, such that it was— small but good—played the school song.

Nathan had caught a ride with a friend, and Jenny had stayed at school longer than she meant to. Now she had to hurry to get back in time for the principal's big kick off welcoming speech. It was always the same speech each year, and Jenny could probably recite most of it from memory.

She slipped into a pair of khaki shorts and a white knit sleeveless top. It would stay in the nineties for most of the evening. She dug into her closet for her favorite pair of sandals, vowing once again that she would clean out her closet and get it organized. Maybe this weekend, she promised herself without much conviction.

She glanced up and saw the old wooden box tucked on the top shelf. The memory box she rarely allowed herself to open, but couldn't bear to throw out. It held all the memories of her high school days with Clay. Except for the most important memory, the one where they made love for the first time. She gave into the wave of nostalgia and allowed herself to go back to the summer day so long ago.

The day had been hot and they had snuck off to the stream behind Greta's house to wade and splash in the cool water. She could remember what she had worn, a lightweight print sundress and sandals.

The sun bounced off of Clay's hair making it glisten where the drops of water clung to it. She splashed him again and again.

"You better watch out, girl. Payback will be ugly." Clay swooped his cupped hand down to the water and flung an arc of icy cold water at her.

She screamed and tried to back away, kicking the water in an effort to drench him again. When she went to swing her foot again, she lost her balance, and Clay reached out and caught her. They both landed in the stream.

"You hurt?"

"I'm on top of you." She grinned at him. "Are you hurt?"

"Hmm... no. And I'm quite aware you're on top of me." He placed his hand behind her head and lowered her face to his. His warm lips teased hers, the heat of his touch and his kisses mixing strangely with the cool of the stream water.

She kissed him back. She loved kissing him. He had a way of making all her senses jangle and she lost all rational thought.

Clay groaned. "You're driving me crazy, girl."

"I like that." Her words came out in a rush.

He sat up in the stream, pulling her with him. "Your dress is all wet."

"Um, hm."

"We should take it off and put it in the sun to dry."

She raised her eyebrow. "Should we?"

"It's only right. I mean, you don't want to go home sopping wet and explain *that* to your father."

He had a point there.

She wanted to *want* him to stop... but she didn't. She wanted him to continue. She'd waited a year for the right time to make love to him. The time felt right now. She loved him and wanted to show him just how much.

He looked at her questioningly. When she didn't ask him to stop, he stood up and pulled her to her feet, never letting go. He picked her up and carefully crossed the rocky stream bed and set her down under the willow tree. She stood next to him, feasting on his glistening skin. He trailed his hands up and down her arms. Slowly. Torturously. She took in a quick breath, her heart hammering, afraid and excited at the same time.

"Are you sure, Jenns?"

She looked into his steel blue eyes, on fire with desire now. Desire for her. It was a heady feeling to see that look in his eyes. She *was* sure.

"I'm sure."

The memory started to fade away, softened a tad, like an old, worn photograph. The present called her name, robbing her of her sweet memories.

* * * * *

Jenny stood in the kitchen, trying to thrust away the glimmers of her past with Clay. Her skin still burned from allowing herself to indulge in the memory of the first time he'd made love to her, but she wasn't going to think about it again. Not ever. That was then, and this was now.

She grabbed the picnic basket from the pantry and loaded it full of food. Extra brownies for her past students who always came by her blanket and said hi. A small cooler of water and soda and she was ready to head out the door. She paused to pat Choo Choo—the black lab mix dog that Nathan had named when he was just five years old. She glanced at the dog's water bowl to make sure he had enough water to survive this heat and she really was out the door.

She pulled into the field beside the school that served as overflow parking for events such as this, which worked fine unless they were having a heavy rainstorm. When that happened, the field flooded and parking was impossible. She grabbed the basket, cooler, and blanket, wishing Nathan would appear to help her. She headed for the oak tree where she always spread her blanket, ever since she had been a young girl attending the school herself.

Nathan caught up with her halfway across the field.

"Hey, Mom, let me get some of that for you."

Her son rescued the food, of course, then the cooler. She smiled at him. He was wearing shorts and a t-shirt, his tan arms and legs giving him a healthy glow of never-ending youth. The invincible young, with their whole lives spread out in front of them. She just hoped the rest of his life would be a little easier than this first part. A boy shouldn't lose his father at such a young age.

He hadn't. Her mind mocked her thoughts. His father was alive and well and in close proximity. Now Nathan was going to have to deal with yet another blow. This week.

"Let's go drop this stuff off and head over to the football field."

"To hear Principal Kohr make the same speech he gives every year?" Her son looked dubious, undoubtedly thinking he could scare up something more exciting.

They crossed to the grove of trees beside the field. Nathan knew the routine well by now. He knew exactly where they were heading and where she wanted to sit. She paused to say hi to a student she had in her class last year, then turned to catch up with Nathan. And came to a dead stop.

Clay, his daughters, and Greta were sitting on some blankets under *her* tree. But it was her spot. She hadn't planned on sharing it with them, but then she realized it was where she and Clay had always picnicked together at Festival Days. Except for her senior year, when her father had forbidden her to see Clay, and Greta had decided she and Clay would sit somewhere else. Not that it had stopped them from meeting behind the school for a few stolen moments.

Jenny sucked in a deep breath, pasted on a smile, and continued on to the grove of trees. Nathan had already plopped down beside Danielle and was carrying on an animated discussion with both girls.

She could almost feel Clay's eyes on her as she approached the old oak. "Hey, Greta. Good to see you. Hi, Clay."

"Jenny, you look wonderful, as always. Hope you don't mind us joining you at your spot? Danielle arranged to meet up here with Nathan." Greta explained.

It appeared Jenny was the only one who didn't know about this rendezvous. She smiled smoothly, sure she was betraying none of her apprehension.

"No, that's fine." Jenny could fib with the best of them when needed. Heck, let's be real, she'd told the biggest whopper of all. Now it was mocking her every day she kept it from Clay.

"Hey, Abigail. Danielle. How are you girls doing?"

"Just fine, Mrs. Bouchard." Danielle answered and Abigail nodded. They immediately turned their attention back to Nathan, who was telling them some exaggerated tale or another. He was the ultimate storyteller.

Clay got up and helped her spread her blanket right next to theirs. "Let me help you get settled." He grabbed the picnic basket and cooler from where Nathan had dropped them and placed them at the edge of the blanket.

Jenny sank down on the blanket for a few minutes' rest before she needed to make her way to the football field.

"It's strange, being back here at the picnic after all these years. The same, yet different." Clay pointed to the new tennis courts. "Those are new. And the track has a new running surface. They built more bleachers at the football field, too."

"The school has really grown since we were here. They keep adding new things, they built a grade school and junior high about ten years ago. One stop shopping for all your child's educational needs. The high school has doubled in size, too. A lot of people moved to the area and commute into New Orleans now."

"Not quite the sleepy little private school it used to be."

"Oh, in a lot of ways it's the same. A lot of the same traditions—like this back-to-school picnic. It's still a tough curriculum and is considered one of the better schools around."

Yes, it was still the same in a lot of ways, like the locker she'd had right across the hall from Clay's. The back stacks at the library, where she'd slip off to meet him. The table at the cafeteria where they sat and had lunch with Joseph and whoever he had been dating at the time. The football field where she watched Clay play football, until he dropped off the team his senior year and said he wasn't interested in the sport any more. That had been strange. She hadn't ever figured that one out. He had loved football.

Just then, a couple of girls from her last year's class came up to where they were sitting. "Hi, Mrs. Bouchard."

"Hi, girls. Did you have a nice summer?"

"The best. But it wasn't long enough." The girls reached out and took the brownies she offered them.

"Girls, this is Dr. Miller, and his daughters, Abigail and Danielle. They are here visiting their grandmother, Mrs. Miller."

"Hi!" The girls looked at Abigail who was just about their age. Abigail nodded to them.

"Hi, Mrs. Miller. We miss you at school. Are you going to substitute teach some this year?"

"Thank you, girls. Probably." Greta smiled at them.

"Hey, Abigail, you want to come over to the football field with us and hear the speeches? They're kind of boring, but then the football guys come on the field and the cheerleaders. That's fun."

Abigail's face lit up and she jumped up, turning a questioning look towards her father. Clay looked conflicted. He stood up, rubbed a hand over his chin, clearly in a moment of indecision.

"How about Danielle and I go over there now too?" Nathan jumped in. Bless the boy for picking up on Clay's hesitance.

Clay nodded. Danielle and Nathan stood up. Nathan and Clay, side by side. Clay flashed an easy smile at Nathan, thanking him silently for his help.

Greta choked on her drink. Jenny turned her attention to the woman and saw her staring at Nathan and Clay. Looking at Nathan, then Clay. Then back again to Nathan.

"You okay, Mom?"

"I'm—yes. No. I mean yes." Greta continued to stare at them. Then Jenny watched as Greta turned and pinned a look on her. At that very point in time, Jenny was pretty darn sure Greta had some major questions, but she didn't say a word.

"Go on, kids, I'm okay. Just swallowed wrong." Greta assured everyone.

Abigail joined her new friends, and Danielle and Nathan trailed behind them. They all headed off towards the field.

"I think I'll go wander around and say hi to some of my friends." Greta got up, with one more look at Jenny, and left.

Jenny was stuck sitting there with Clay. The man she had told to stay away from her, the one whose mom was probably close to figuring out her secret. She needed to tell Clay the truth. And soon. Or someone else was going to notice, and gossip spread like wildfire through Comfort Crossing, Mississippi.

* * * * *

Clay found himself surrounded by confusing females these days. His mom had acted no less than terribly strange just now, and Jenny looked pale and frightened half to death.

"Jenns?"

"Hm?"

"You okay? You don't look very good. Is the heat getting to you?"

The heat. Good excuse. "A little."

"You want to stay here, or head over to the field?"

"I really do need to go over and hear Principal Kohr's speech and watch the parade."

Clay nodded in agreement. He automatically reached a hand down to help Jenny to her feet. She hesitated then reached up.

When her hand slipped into his, a feeling of instant heat rocked through his belly. He grasped her small hand in his and gently pulled her to her feet. He looked down at that hand in his. So familiar. So strange. He squeezed it tightly for a moment, fighting the urge to pull it close and rest it on his chest, to press it up to his lips like he'd done so many times in his life.

She snatched her hand away, her eyes flashing with the same conflicting emotions he was feeling. There was no way she could hide that from him. He knew her too well. She stood there, looking deep into his eyes, as everyone and everything around them faded away. They were back in time, when the future was theirs for the asking.

"Hi, Mrs. Bouchard." A cute little girl with braids came up to them. "I'll miss you this year."

"Hello, Morgan. I'll miss you too, but I bet you'll like third grade."

The moment was broken. Reality crashed back on him.

"I bet we'll get too much homework."

He watched as Jenny offered the girl an encouraging smile. "Well, do your best on it."

"I will, Mrs. Bouchard." The girl turned and skipped off in the direction of the field.

"Ready?" Jenny's voice held a please-don't-bother-me tone.

"You know, sometime we're going to have to sit down and talk about it."

"About what?" Her voice was edged in panic.

"About what's still between us. How we feel."

Instead of being panicked about his remark, he'd swear she looked relieved.

"There isn't anything still between us." Jenny lied to him. Her eyes held the truth. She felt the same feelings he did. Her eyes couldn't lie. She'd never been able to lie to him.

* * * * *

Jenny felt an enormous wave of relief wash over her. He wanted to talk about them. She and Clay. Nothing about Nathan. She'd seen the look in Greta's eyes and was worried Clay was going to start to have questions. She needed to have answers for him. She just didn't know how to tell him. Where to start, or how to find the words. There was no future for her and Clay, no matter if there were still feelings swirling beneath the surface. No way could she have a relationship with him, after the secret she'd kept.

If only—she stopped her thoughts cold. She wasn't going to start on the if-only game. But she needed to keep Clay and Nathan apart for now, until she found the right time to tell them both. It wasn't safe for people to see them standing side by side. Someone else was going to notice, especially when Nathan even had some of Clay's mannerisms.

She snatched a deep breath, trying to focus on what she had to do. And what she shouldn't do. Her world was once again cantering out of control. It seemed like it had been that way since Joseph died. Just when she thought she was getting her feet under her, it had skidded out of control again.

Clay was standing there looking at her, searching her face, questioning her with his eyes. But she had no answers, and no idea how she was going to deal with the truth. But she did know how to avoid. Classic Avoidance 101 should be a required course for all females.

"Let's head over to the field." She turned her back on Clay and set off at a brisk pace, ignoring the heat, ignoring the crowds, determined to find them seats as far away from Nathan as possible.

She found seats at the near end of the field. She could see Nathan and Danielle talking to a group of high school students down by the track. Perfect.

To her horror, she saw Nathan look up, spot her and wave. She waved back – a tiny, reluctant gesture. *Don't come up here.*

"Look, there are the kids." Clay waved a broad stroke through the air. Danielle waved back and held up a just a minute sign. She tugged on Nathan's sleeve and pointed up to Jenny and Clay.

It took everything in Jenny's control to keep from shaking her head no, or speaking it out loud.

Nathan took Danielle's elbow and started to lead her up the bleachers. Jenny wanted to scream. She thought of saying she was sick and Nathan should drive her home. The thought of running away was tantalizingly appealing right now. She looked for storm clouds or, better yet, a hurricane. Nothing and no one was going to stop this.

She jumped up. "Nathan, come sit by your ol' mom. I never see you anymore."

Nathan looked at her strangely, but came and sat next to her, rather than next to Clay. But there she was, the only defense between the two males. She leaned forward in her seat, trying to cut off the two of them.

She caught sight of Greta, watching from the bottom of the bleachers. Looking. Staring. Questioning.

"Nathan, I'm not feeling well. Must be the heat. You think you could walk me back to the blanket?" The heck with the unwritten rule that teachers must sit through opening speeches and the parade.

"Mom, I have to walk with the football team. I need to go down to the field in a few minutes."

"I'll walk you back." Clay interrupted.

She scrambled for a new excuse. "No, that's okay."

"Danielle, you keep an eye on your sister, okay?"

"Sure, Dad."

Well, at least Clay and Nathan would be apart, not sitting together out in the open. Her breathing sped up.

"You do look pale," Clay said.

She felt like the world was crashing down around her, like a student caught cheating on an exam. "Yes, let's go." Jenny got up and hurried down the bleachers, narrowly escaping the hand Clay held out to help her.

* * * * *

Clay settled back against the oak tree and enjoyed the cool of the shade. There was not a hint of a breeze this evening and the humid evening air hung oppressively around them. Jenny pressed a can of pop against her forehead. She snagged a piece of ice and ran it up and down her slender throat. His reaction was immediate, bringing back so many regrets in his life. So many choices he'd made. The one fateful one, when he had broken up with Jenny. Not that he'd had any choice regarding the break up, but she didn't know that. Jenny's father had threatened to have Clay's mother fired from her teaching job, and Clay had no doubt the man would have accomplished it. Jenny's father was on the school board. He had managed to get Clay's scholarship to the private high school pulled his senior year, there was no doubt Old Man Delacroix could get his mom fired.

Greta had tutored extra students and Clay quit sports and took an after-school job, along with the weekend job he already had. They had managed to scrape by and borrow enough money to get him through his last year.

After his mom had worked so hard for him, there was no way Clay was going to let Jenny's old man take his mom's job away. Then, right as Clay left for college, Jenny's old man had thrown in the deciding factor. He had threatened to cut Jenny off completely. No money, no help with her college fees, nothing.

So Clay had done what he felt he had to. He'd broken up with Jenny. No one stood up to Old Man Delacroix and survived.

Jenny's voice pulled him from his thoughts.

"Clay, we need to talk." Jenny picked up another ice cube and he swore he was going to snatch it away from her before he'd let her torture him again by slowly rubbing it down her bare arms.

"Okay, let's talk." *If it makes you drop that darn ice cube.*

"Not here. Not around everyone. Can we meet somewhere tomorrow?"

"I could pick you up tomorrow after work. I have to go into New Orleans and pick up some research material from the medical library on a disease I think one of my patients has. The library could send them, but I don't really want to wait for that. Besides, I haven't been to the French Quarter in years. I thought I might go eat there after I get the files I need. I'm craving a muffuletta and fried onion rings, followed closely by beignets and chicory coffee at Café Du Monde. You feel like tagging along?"

She paused in her icy torture of his restraint. "That sounds good. I haven't been to New Orleans in a long time either."

He watched as she slowly resumed rubbing the ice cube along the back of her neck. The water dripped down her skin in narrow rivulets of moisture. He knew one thing for sure. They'd go somewhere that didn't have ice cubes.

Chapter Six

The next day, Becky Lee made a picnic lunch and invited Jenny and Izzy to the park for a quick get together. Izzy's boys, Timmy and Jeremy, ran around with their friends, while the women sat at a table in the gazebo at the city park.

Jenny reached out and took a half of a chicken salad sandwich on home baked bread. "This looks great, Becky Lee."

"Becky Lee is the best cook in the county." Izzy reached for the fresh fruit tray.

Becky Lee was pretty sure her friends were biased when it came to her cooking, but she really did enjoy it. She was always experimenting with some new recipe. Wouldn't hurt Jenny to eat more, and Izzy too for that matter. Both of them had dropped weight, due to the stress of the last few years.

Izzy sat in the shade, the light breeze blowing her

golden red hair. She kept an eye on her boys as they played on the playground. It was good to see Izzy looking so relaxed and happy. It had been a long time since she'd looked that way. This new man she was dating, Owen, seemed to be good for her.

"Have you seen Owen recently?" Becky Lee asked.

"He's out of town, went back to Chicago for about a week. Had some business to attend to." Izzy's face held a wistful look.

"Ah, ha. You miss him, don't you?" Jenny joined in. "I knew you were falling for him."

"I don't know if I'm falling for him, or whatever you'd call it. But I do enjoy spending time with him."

"How is he with the boys?" Jenny asked.

"Well, he's a bit overwhelmed, I think. He's not used to kids... and my boys are, well... boys." Izzy grinned. "Owen is getting quite an education on children this summer. Between Jake's cousins' kids and my boys, he's getting a crash course in the chaos that is kids."

"Has your ex finished giving you trouble?" Becky Lee asked.

"I'm not sure Rick will ever be over having an opinion on how I live my life, but I don't have to listen to him anymore."

Becky Lee turned to Jenny. "So, you're really going to go into New Orleans for dinner with Clay?" Becky Lee wasn't sure that was the best idea Jenny had ever had.

"Yes. I need to talk to him. It's time. I appreciate that

you two kept my secret for so long. I never would have made it through all this without you. But it's time for Clay to know the truth about Nathan." Jenny sighed and pushed her hair away from her face. "I dread telling Nathan, too."

"You know we're always here for you," Izzy said. "We support whatever decision you make."

"I know. You two are the best. It's just time for the truth to come out. I just worry about the consequences, both with Clay and with Nathan. Not to mention Joseph's parents. I'm not sure I would have done it differently. I was so young when I got pregnant with Nathan, and so afraid of what my father would do. But now it's my mess to straighten out."

Izzy leaned over and gave Jenny a hug. "It's going to be rough for a bit, but we'll help you through it."

"You can call me when you get home tonight. No matter how late it is and let me know how it went. I can come over if you need me." Becky Lee didn't want her friend sitting alone at her house all upset. She was sure that Clay was going to use that steel cold anger on Jenny, and her friend would not be able to withstand much of that. She admitted that Clay had a right to be angry, but he was the one who had insisted he wanted to be free and broke up with Jenny. Becky Lee had sided with Jenny when she said she was going to keep Nathan's father a secret. Jenny hadn't wanted Clay to marry her out of obligation.

It was funny how it had worked out. Joseph said he'd marry her to give a name to the baby, and they'd stay married for a bit. But then, somehow, they had become a family. A happy family, at that. Becky Lee had actually been a bit jealous of them. They seemed to have the perfect life. Well, until it all fell apart.

"And I'll call you in the morning after I get the boys to summer day camp."

"Really, I'll be okay. I think worrying about telling him is even worse than the actual telling. Well, maybe." Jenny's face held a wry smile. "Or maybe not. But I'll tell you one thing, I'll be glad to have the secret out in the open. I'm tired of keeping it. I'm pretty sure Greta has figured it out. I was young and scared before. I'm an adult now, and it's time."

Becky Lee admired Jenny's strength and resolve. She reached across the picnic table and squeezed Jenny's hand. "It's going to be okay. It's all going to work out."

Becky Lee just hoped she was right.

* * * * *

Jenny felt like a school girl again. She had spent the day agonizing over what to wear, and had tried on ten different outfits. What was the proper outfit to wear to tell your ex-lover he is the father of your son? Their son. That he *had* a son. Where was she going to find the right words? And the right outfit, for that matter. At least Nathan was taking Choo Choo and spending the night with Joseph's parents, so she wouldn't have to come home and face her son on the same night she faced Clay. Nathan and Joseph's parents would have one more night before she blew apart their lives.

She looked up at the memory box, sitting on the high shelf in her closet. Part of her wanted to take it out and look through the contents. She rarely indulged herself. It had been a few years, now, since she had opened it. She could picture the ticket stubs to the first movie she and Clay had gone to. A handful of wrinkled notes he had written her. Photographs. Pressed flowers. A bracelet he had given her. She had even kept a few things that Nathan had made when he was little and a photograph of Nathan each year on his birthday, from age one until the year Joseph had died, guilty that Clay had missed all those birthdays.

No, there wasn't time for that. She needed to get ready. She sighed and picked up a simple red sundress. The weather was threatening to break the record high. The air conditioner barely made a dent in the sultry heat in the old house. She loved the house, with its big old windows and wrap around porch. She'd updated the kitchen to stainless steel appliances and new cabinets and countertops. The rest of the house she'd left exactly as they'd found it when she and Joseph had gone house hunting, all those years ago. The worn wooden floors, the clawfoot bathtub in the master bath. She loved the house, even though it seemed hauntingly empty with Joseph gone. She had considered moving to something smaller, but she just couldn't give up the house where Joseph had shown so much love to her son.

She held up the sundress and stood in front of the full length mirror. She wondered what Clay thought about her now. Did he think she looked old? Even she could see the stress of the last year had taken its toll. A few gray hairs filtered through her otherwise chestnut brown hair. There were wrinkles at the sides of her eyes now, that made her look tired. She was tired. Joseph's death, and now the stress of knowing she had to tell Clay the truth, it all showed on her face. No amount of miracle lotion the infomercials touted could take that away. Plus, her life was only going to get more stressful after the truth came out.

She dusted on baby power in an effort to stay cool in the humidity, and slipped on the sundress. She reached up and deftly pulled her hair back in a French braid, anything to keep cooler. The image she saw in her full length mirror showed a tired woman, a stressed woman with tiny wrinkles at the edges of her eyes. She shook her head and crossed to the closet. After rummaging around for a comfortable pair of sandals for walking around the French Quarter, she gave herself one quick last look. It would have to do.

She had it all planned out. They'd have a nice drive over. It only took about an hour to drive into New Orleans. Clay would get the medical information he needed, then they would go to the French Quarter.

They'd eat at a small corner café, outside, if it cooled off enough. Then, after coffee at Cafe Du Monde, they'd walk along the river. Then she'd tell him.

She paused and wanted to smack her forehead with a great big *duh*. Suddenly she knew the flaw in her plan. The fatal flaw. If she told him the truth when they were in New Orleans, she'd be an hour away from home. She'd either have to ride back with a furious Clay, or call someone to come and get her. This wasn't going to work out. She needed to be somewhere safe when she told him. Somewhere she'd be able to get away from his fury.

She hurried over to the phone to punch in his number. She'd cancel going with him tonight. She'd tell him tomorrow. Somewhere close to home.

Before she could get the last number punched in, she saw Clay pull into her driveway. He leveraged his tall frame out of the car and crossed the distance to the porch with long easy strides. She felt trapped. How to get out of it now? She crossed over to the door and opened it to his knock.

"Hey, Jenny, ready to go?"

She paused, not sure what to say.

"Something wrong?" Clay looked so handsome, standing there in her doorway, dressed in khaki slacks and a blue knit shirt that brought out the deep lapis-blue flecks in his eyes.

She couldn't come up with one plausible excuse to give him for why she needed to cancel. "No, nothing's wrong. Let me find my keys." She picked up her bag again and fished out her keys.

"So you're locking doors now?"

"Ever since Joseph…" She paused while she struggled with the key in the lock. "Well I just feel safer locking the doors now."

"I keep telling Mom she should lock her doors, but she says she never has, and never will."

Jenny wrestled with the lock until she heard the familiar click. "Okay, all set."

She might as well go with him. Who knows, maybe they'd even have fun in the Quarter. Maybe she'd get to know this older Clay and figure out the best way to tell him. And, the truth be told, she could use a night out. A night of no responsibility, of talk and laughter. She could have that one night with Clay, couldn't she? She could treat herself to that one little luxury. She promised herself that all thoughts of telling the truth were buried for the night. She was just going to have a good time. Tomorrow she'd tell Clay. She promised.

* * * * *

He'd promised himself he was just taking Jenny along for a good time, like he'd go out with any of his friends. But there she was, standing in the doorway in that red dress, and it almost took his breath away. She looked so fabulous in red. Always had.

She stood there on her porch in the sassy red dress, looking expectantly at him, and he stood there like a fool.

He cleared his throat and found his voice. "Jenns, you look good."

"Thanks." She looked at him tentatively, as if she were unsure if he meant it or not.

He grinned at her. "Really good, Jenns."

She smiled at him then. Her warm, sunny, just-for-him smile. The one he remembered. It tugged at him. Tonight he wanted a night of fun, of no responsibility. No worrying about Claire leaving, Abigail talking, Danielle getting into trouble. Just fun. He'd planned ahead and talked to the doctor in the neighboring town about taking emergency call for him tonight. So, for about twelve hours he was a free man.

"Let's go." He opened the car door for her and watched as she slid inside, one long leg balancing while she maneuvered in. She had great legs. Always had. Still did. Was that going to be a theme of his thoughts tonight?

He closed the door and went around to the driver's side of the car, sucking in the humid air, trying to fight off the instant attraction. Though instant attraction was really the wrong turn of phrase to use for a woman he'd known for twenty years. But it was there. The way her hand rested gently on the car door as she slid inside. He glanced at her long, graceful fingers. Magic fingers, he used to call them. They could make his skin dance and heat him to a burn with one small touch.

He climbed in and started the car. The faint scent of baby powder floated across the seat. She still used baby powder. She was going to drive him mad. He cleared his throat again. "All set?"

He drove into New Orleans while they talked about the weather, and the school where Jenny taught. The tension in the air slowly drifted away with the miles. He talked about working at the clinic and how Velda was saving his life. She told stories of her students. He regaled her with tales of his life as an intern. She told him all about her house. It was obvious how much she loved it. He ignored the fact she had lived there with Joseph. He just focused on the present, being with Jenny. Talking and laughing like they used to.

He pulled into the visitors' parking lot at Tulane and ran in to get the research information he needed. As he walked the hallways, he couldn't help the memories that came back to haunt him.

The weekend when Jenny came to Tulane to surprise him, his first weekend of college, he'd been so happy to see her. A fact he forced himself to hide immediately. He'd done the only thing possible. He'd broken up with her. Convinced her he wanted to be free to date, to be a normal college kid. Free. Just like her father ordered. A bargain with the devil.

He could still remember the look on Jenny's face. Her eyes had filled with tears, but she hadn't allowed them to run free. He had barely been able to breathe. Barely been able to keep from reaching out and holding her, telling her he was sorry and it was all a lie. Reassuring her that he loved her.

She'd yelled at him. Argued with him. Then, finally, she'd quietly reached out to touch his face, but he'd caught her hand and pushed it away. If he had let that hand touch him, he would have been lost.

She had stood there, abnormally pale, trembling. She'd snatched her hand free, turned, and walked away without saying another word. That had been the last time he'd spoken to Jenny before this week.

As he had watched her walk away, all that long time ago, he had vowed to win her back. To get through medical school and prove to Jenny, her father, and everyone in Comfort Crossing that he was good enough for Jenny Delacroix. She was his future. He had thought he just had to put his future on hold for a few years. But it hadn't worked out like that.

Life had a way of throwing curves when he wasn't looking. He had never even thought Joey had a thing for Jenny, when they all used to run around together. Joey was always dating one cheerleader or another. Never anyone steady. Oh, he and Jenns had been close friends, but nothing more. Then, bang, he married Jenny just weeks after the breakup. It didn't seem right. But it must have worked for them. Obviously. They had a child and remained married all these years.

Clay pushed the memories away. Back where they didn't hurt so badly. Tonight was not a night for memories and regrets.

He hurried back out to the car and Jenny, sitting there waiting for him. In her red dress with her incredibly sexy legs, and her dancing eyes.

She flashed him a smile when he opened the car door. He dropped the research into the backseat and started the car. "Let's go."

He found a parking space at a garage at the west end of the French Quarter and gave the keys to the attendant. He took Jenny's arm and they headed out into the busyness that was the French Quarter.

He took her elbow and tucked her safely against his side, placing himself between the street and Jenny. They headed down Iberville, then cut across Bourbon Street for a few blocks. Music tumbled out of the open doorways and windows. People strolled along the streets with drinks and laughter. The smell of Cajun cooking drifted out the open doors of a corner restaurant. A boy stood on the corner with bottle caps stuck on the bottom of his shoes, tap dancing for the passing crowd in hopes of earning some spare change.

Jenny tugged at his sleeve. "Look, frozen daiquiris. Can I get one?" He watched Jenny delight in looking at the churning daiquiri machines with their clear glass fronts, beckoning in a rainbow of colors. After considering her flavor options, she decided on raspberry lemon and sipped it as they cut across to Decatur Street and ended up in Jackson Square.

The square bustled with musicians and magicians,

fortune tellers and painters. A man juggled in a ring of fire. Horse drawn carriages lined the street and the air rang with the clop, clop of their hoofs on the street as they slowly pulled carriages of couples taking in the sights.

"Want to sit here for a bit and people watch?" Clay asked.

"Yes." Jenny sank down on the steps. She stretched out her legs in front of her and slipped off her sandals, balancing her heels on them. Jenny and her bare feet. She had always loved going barefoot and painting her toenails in bright splashes of color. Tonight was no exception, her nails were painted bright red to match her dress.

Clay sat down beside her and they quietly watched the people drift by. A couple walked by with a little boy of about two years, his hand clenched firmly around the string of a balloon. A policeman on horseback rested at the corner, watching over the milling crowd. A man across from them, leaning against a railing, started strumming his guitar and singing a haunting melody about love lost.

"See that couple over there?" Jenny pointed at a young couple arguing about twelve feet away from them. "He just forgot their anniversary. Their first anniversary. She's not going to be consoled with some lame bunch of flowers, it's going to take more than that. I mean, considering he went out with the guys and played poker last night, and now this."

Clay laughed. He'd forgotten their game of so many years ago, making up stories as they people watched. "See that guy painting pictures? He studied in Paris. Lived in a garret. Then a great art critic panned his first exhibition. He moved here and sells his paintings in the shops around here, and to tourists walking through the square. He lives in a dilapidated, one-room efficiency apartment, over a bar on Iberville. The lady who owns it gives him his meals for free for helping her clean the bar after closing."

Jenny pointed across the square. "See that old man? He's been a widower for twenty years. It's his anniversary today, too. They would have been married fifty years today. He comes back to this very spot every year because this is where he proposed to her. Right here in Jackson Square."

Clay jumped in. "He bought her flowers back then and a small simple wedding band. No money for a diamond. But she didn't need one."

"She was so happy. The happiest day of her life. She'd tell the story over and over again to her children."

Clay pointed to a young man on the corner. "See him? His hot date stood him up and he's ticked. He's never been stood up before."

"It's probably good for him. He looks entirely too cocky." Jenny laughed and flashed her dazzling just-for-him smile. It took his breath away. Again.

He glanced across the square to a lone woman sitting and sipping a cup of coffee. "See her? She has a deep dark secret. There's someone she should tell it to, but she can't bring herself to tell the truth."

Jenny choked on her daiquiri.

"You okay?"

She stared at the woman across the square with what he'd swear was a look of empathy, then she shook her head. "Yeah, sure." She slipped on her sandals, jumped up and tugged at his hand. "Come on! I'm starved. Let's go eat."

* * * * *

Jenny loved the little café they found, with wooden bench booths right next to the hurricane doors thrown open wide. The ceiling fans kept the dark room comfortable. They ate muffuletta, that Clay said he had been craving, made of wonderful round Italian bread stuffed with meats and cheese and a spicy olive vinegar dressing. They split an order of onion rings and chased it all down with ice cold beer.

She was feeling young and alive and carefree, feelings she hadn't indulged in since she couldn't remember when. But she liked the way she felt. She liked talking and laughing with Clay.

"Ready for beignets?"

"Is it getting too late?"

"Not a chance. I'm not missing beignets for anything. Besides, I have emergency coverage for the patients. Let's stay out late and ignore the world."

"That, Clay Miller, is one of the best ideas you've had."

They strolled over to Café du Monde for beignets and chicory coffee. The night sky darkened, but the lights of the Quarter just got brighter. More people filtered into the Quarter as the night went on.

"I'm stuffed." Jenny pushed back from the sticky table where powdered sugar from the fried beignets had fallen all over the table top. She dipped her hand in her glass of ice water, grabbed an ice cube, and started to clean off her sticky hands.

Clay looked at her strangely.

"What's wrong?"

"Nothing." He didn't sound convinced. He still looked distraught and stared at her cleaning up the powdered sugar off of her hands. She'd swear he was staring at the ice cube.

He cleared his throat. "Let's go walk along the river."

They walked up the ramp from Café du Monde and crossed the railroad tracks over to the walkway along the river. It was a beautiful summer night and couples walked along the river, or sat on the benches scattered along the shore. Jenny tugged Clay's hand and led him over to a bench. They sat down and watched a barge navigate the ninety degree turn in the river, going upstream against the current.

It felt good just sitting there with Clay and watching the river. She instinctively leaned back against him. Then she realized what she had done, and sat up straight.

She felt his warm gentle hand on her shoulder. "It's okay, Jenns. Lean back. Watch the river. Get comfortable."

She did lean back against him, and he slowly stroked her arm. She wasn't even sure if he was aware he was doing it. He looked lost in his thoughts.

She could hear his slow steady breathing. Feel his heart beating. Feel his breath softly brush across her shoulder. She could get lost in this moment too, if she'd just let herself.

"I don't want this night to end." Jenny couldn't believe she said the thought out loud. She sure hadn't meant to.

* * * * *

Clay turned her so he could see her face. He wasn't ready for this night to end either. "Let's not end it."

"It's a long drive back, Clay."

"So we'll stay. Let's go back to the Quarter. Grab a drink and sit outside. I'll get us rooms. We'll stay up too late and regret it tomorrow. How about it?"

Jenny looked unsure. He could see her fighting between what she wanted to do and what she thought she should do.

"Two rooms, Jenny. Say we can stay."

She smiled up at him then. "Let's do it. Let's be irresponsible and stay up late. Let's drink into the early morning hours. And we'll complain all the way back to Comfort Crossing in the morning."

He laughed then, feeling more alive than he had in years. He got up and pulled her to her feet. "Let's go find rooms, then let's find some place to sit and listen to the music."

He found them two rooms at The Marie, an old boutique hotel he could see charmed Jenny as soon as they walked in the door. He got them two rooms, and Jenny insisted on going up to freshen up, whatever it was that women did when they freshened up. He didn't mind. He was taking great pleasure in seeing Jenny enjoy herself. They rode a rickety elevator up to the third floor, and he found their rooms. He opened the door to Jenny's room for her and went inside with her.

"Give me a minute." She crossed over to the tiny bathroom and he could hear water running. He made a quick call to his mother to tell her he was spending the night in the Quarter. She didn't sound a bit surprised, and told him to enjoy himself.

He went over to the French doors on the far side of the room and opened the doors onto a balcony and stepped outside. He heard her come up behind him. Felt her warmth.

"A balcony." She clapped her hands in delight.

He looked down on the tiny courtyard below them. The courtyard was deserted. Low lights illuminated a small pool in the brick courtyard. "Too bad we don't have our swim suits, though that didn't used to stop us…"

"Clay Miller!"

"Sorry." He knew he didn't sound one bit sorry.

"Let's go sit down there and get a bottle of wine from the bar. Come on." She was tugging at his hand again, like Abigail did when she was excited.

"All right. Let's go."

* * * * *

Jenny settled down in the lounge chair in the charming open air courtyard. Subtle music drifted into the courtyard from a nearby jazz club. The courtyard sparkled with low lying lights strung along the walkway. Cool blue lights in the pool threw refractions of rippled lighting across the surface of the water. The quiet voices of a couple on a balcony at the far end of the courtyard floated down on the still night air. The fountain in the corner of the courtyard bubbled its soothing melody. Jenny exhaled a sigh of contentment. It was one of those singularly perfect moments in life, as far as he was concerned.

Clay handed her a glass of wine then lowered his tall frame to the chair beside hers. "Now *this* is nice."

"Who knew you could find quiet spots like this in the middle of the French Quarter?"

"It is nice to get away. I'm glad you decided to stay."

"I am, too." She smiled at him, took a sip of wine, and put her feet up on a footstool. "So, do you like being a doctor?"

"I do." Clay stared at the wine glass in his hand. "But

the funny thing is—and I don't know if it's just because I'm doing something new and different—I really like working in Doc Baker's office. It's a whole different world of medicine than my practice in Boston."

"I'm glad you're enjoying it."

"That Velda is a life saver. She knows everyone. She balances like ten things at once and never blinks an eye."

"Doc Baker always jokes it's really Velda's clinic."

"It is. She is always in a friendly, upbeat mood. She remembers everything that's happened to everyone. It's nice, working there. At my Boston practice there's no end of politics going on. It's not only the nurses working there either. The doctors are the worst. Arguing about percentages and this and that. It gets old."

"How many partners do you have?"

"Five. No, four now." Clay looked at her with sad eyes. "One left with Claire, so to speak. My own partner and my wife."

"I'm sorry, Clay."

"I am, too. But obviously he wasn't the only problem we had. Claire was never really happy. I just wasn't who or what she wanted me to be."

No, he'd never been what Claire wanted. He knew that now. After he heard the news about Jenny's marriage, he'd done the only thing possible. He'd shut off his feelings and thrown himself into his schooling. Then he dated every woman who took his fancy. He'd married Claire just a few months later, when she became pregnant. Still duty bound to do the right thing, he married her even though she had tricked him and secretly gone off the pill. She wanted to marry a medical student with a bright future and she'd picked him. He needed to be a father to his child, so they married and started down a rocky road of misery. Claire was never satisfied with anything. To give her some credit, she knew she never had his heart, and it ate at her every day. So she bought things. Lots of things. From home shopping on cable TV, to weekly shopping forays to the mall. Clay had struggled to pay the bills and get through medical school. He remembered those years as a blur of exhaustion. His one bright spot was his daughter, Danielle, who seemed to make it all worthwhile.

They spent his four years of college, his years of medical school and residency, making each other miserable. Then Claire became pregnant again. Clay persuaded himself to really try at the marriage, but nothing he tried could convince Claire. With the birth of Abigail, Clay had hoped Claire and he could try yet another attempt to make the marriage work, but no such luck.

Jenny's voice pulled him away from his thoughts. "So she gave you custody of the girls?"

"Full custody. I still marvel at my luck. She could have made it ugly, but she just really wants to play with them a few times a year. Go on a whirlwind shopping trip or quick vacation and then she's done with mothering. She deposits them on my doorstep with a kiss and promises about their next fun outing."

"How are the girls with that? I guess it hurts, huh?"

"They try to hide it, though sometimes I think Danielle, at least, is learning to accept Claire at face value, nothing more or nothing less. But it's hard on the girls, knowing their mother doesn't want them to live with her." He leaned forward in his chair and sat sideways, his knees brushing the side of her chair, just inches away from her leg. He wanted to move over just those few inches to connect with her, but he didn't.

He sighed deeply. "But the good thing is I've really gotten to know my girls this last year or so. I had been so busy at work, coming home late, missing their school events and sports. Now there's only me, so they've become my first priority."

"I bet they like that."

"I think they do." He smiled. "Girls are strange creatures. I may never understand them."

"You're not supposed to. They grow up into women, and women want to be mysterious."

"Is that how it works?"

"That's how it works." She sat up and swung her legs next to Clay's. He reached over and placed his hand on her knee, he couldn't help himself.

"I've always been able to talk to you, Jenny. I've missed that."

"I'm sorry you didn't have that with Claire."

"Claire was a lot of things, but my friend? No, never that. How about Joseph? Could you talk to him?"

"Yes, I could. We talked about everything. He was a good friend. Always."

That hurt. It still rocked him to the core that she had married his best friend.

"I'm sorry, Clay."

"No, I'm glad you had a good marriage. I always wanted you to be happy. You were, weren't you?"

"I was." Jenny stood up, obviously uncomfortable discussing how happy she had been, married to Clay's best friend. "I'm getting a little tired, how about you?"

"I guess we'd better get some sleep. Have to hit the road early in the morning."

"Could we stop for beignets and coffee on the way out of town?"

He flashed a smile. "We could do that."

He rested his hand on her arm, leading her out of the courtyard and into the cool paneled lobby. He pressed the elevator button, still keeping his hand on her arm, liking the connection.

The creaking elevator shook and jerked its way up to the third floor, where the doors opened to the moss green carpeted hallway. He led Jenny to her door and silently took her offered door card. He slid it into the lock and opened the door for her.

Then he just stood there, trapped in time. He could hear his breathing, just on the edge of jagged. As she turned to look at him, her eyes burned with a look he remembered so well. He was inches from her, not moving towards her, not moving away.

For a fleeting moment, he thought he was going to kiss her, but then he pulled back slowly. "Goodnight, Jenns. I had a really great time."

He turned, walked the few steps to his room, and slipped inside his door, not sure if he had made a big mistake or a sane decision in not kissing Jenny.

Chapter Seven

Clay had been outside her door at six thirty that morning, just as he promised. His clothes looked unrumpled, as if they had not been slept in, and it hit her with a jolt that he probably hadn't worn them last night. Hadn't worn anything. In the room right next to hers. Her emotions were in overdrive this morning.

"Hey, Jenns, ready for breakfast?"

She stood there, staring at his unwrinkled shirt like a fool. "Yes, um, sure."

His blue eyes were wide awake and flashing with a let's-get-this-day-going look. He'd always been an early morning person, darn it. Full of energy. She was sure she looked bedraggled and tired, though she'd tried her best to repair the damage with what little make up she had in her handbag. She'd brushed her hair and pulled it back. She wished she would have thought to pull off her sundress when she had dropped onto the bed, exhausted, last night. She tried to convince herself it just had the meant-to-be-crinkled look. She glanced down at her dress. *Right. The crinkly look.*

"We'll go grab some beignets and coffee, then head back to Comfort Crossing."

"Sounds good." She gave a quick glance around the hotel room to make sure she hadn't forgotten anything and pulled the door shut.

A few minutes later, they walked out into the warm morning sunshine. A few storekeepers were outside, sweeping off the remains of the revelry from a night in the Quarter. One older man, with gray hair and quick smile, stood outside hosing down the sidewalk in front of his store. He smiled as they stepped into the street to avoid the spray. "Sorry 'bout that."

"No problem." Clay answered.

They made their way to Café du Monde, yet again. Clay ordered up two orders of beignets and two cups of coffee, and the waitress headed inside to place their order.

"I'm glad we stayed last night."

"I am, too. Though you seem to be handling the morning better than I am."

"Jenns, I'm going to make a morning girl out of you someday."

Her heart flipped in her chest. No, he wasn't. Because he was leaving. After he found out the truth.

She'd had such a great time with him last night, getting

to know him again. Watching him smile and laugh and unwind. Her nerves were raw with the emotions surging through her this morning. She had been so sure he was going to bend down and kiss her last night. So positive. But he hadn't. Not that it mattered, since soon he was going to be so furious with her that the chance was gone forever. Did she really want to know what it felt to be kissed by Clay Miller after all this time? Did she want just one more memory seared into her mind?

Yes, darn it all, she *had* wanted to know what it would feel like.

"Jenns? You look lost in thought."

"Um?" But she was saved by the waitress delivering their order.

* * * * *

At five o'clock that evening, there she was again. Right back to where she was last night at this time, holding up clothes in front of the full length mirror. Jenny sighed. She had made plans to meet up with Clay again. She was going to tell him the truth. Tonight.

"Mom?" Nathan stood in the doorway to her room. "You okay?"

"I'm fine."

"You look... funny."

She crossed over and gave her son a quick one armed hug. "I'm fine. Just lost in thought."

"I'm going out to Eddie's tonight. Okay?"

"Are his parents going to be home?"

"Uh, huh. Alexa and some other kids are going to hang out there."

Ah, Alexa, the girl he'd had a crush on for about a year, but had never worked up the nerve to ask out. She smiled to herself. He thought she hadn't figured that out. She didn't know why he hadn't asked Alexa out, because any girl would be lucky to have him.

"And I'm taking Danielle with me to meet some of the kids. Her dad said it was okay. She's kind of cool, in a friend kind of way. I can talk to her."

Clay must feel like he'd gotten to know Nathan a little bit to allow this to happen. "That's fine. But you need to be back by eleven-thirty."

"Mom…"

"No 'moms.' That's plenty late for you to be out in the car. And be good. I'm trusting you on this, Nathan."

Her son stood there, looking incredibly innocent and clean cut. How could this be the same child who had been getting into so much trouble the last few months? Maybe it had just been a phase, a stage that was thankfully over. She could only hope.

She was glad he was getting to be friends with Danielle. His half-sister. He'd find that out soon enough. She turned to face Nathan.

"And Nathan. No drinking. I mean it. None."

"Okay, Mom. I know the rules. And I'll be home by eleven-thirty."

"Have fun, then." She brushed a kiss on his forehead

and he turned and clambered down the stairs. The back door slammed, and she heard the car engine rev up in the driveway. She noticed there was no squealing of tires this time, but she made no promises about when he turned the corner down the street.

Back to deciding what to wear. What to say. What to do.

* * * * *

"Danielle, you're going to drive me crazy if you keep wearing outfits like that. Go upstairs and change." Clay walked into Greta's kitchen just in time to see his daughter come downstairs with one of her impossibly short skirts, stomach showing beneath a short little tank top thingie, with straps that looked barely strong enough to keep the top up.

"Dad"

"I mean it." He watched his daughter flounce out of the kitchen and bang her way upstairs.

"Hey, Mom." He crossed over and gave his mom a quick hug. "Where's Abigail?"

"She's outside playing in the barn. Checking out those new kittens."

"She does seem taken with them. Claire never wanted a pet in the house." Clay reached to swipe a slice of tomato, but Greta was ready for him and swatted his hand away.

"Abigail and I are having sandwiches. Danielle said they were going to get something to eat on the way to

Eddie's."

"I'm still not sure I should have said yes to her going."

"Clay, you have to let her grow up sometime."

"But Nathan has been in trouble recently." He saw Greta raise her eyebrow at him in her you're-being-ridiculous way. "I know, so has Danielle. Don't you think that's a bad combination?"

"I think you need to give them a chance."

"Well, Nathan seemed nice enough at the picnic. And he's great with Abigail."

Just then he heard the sound of a car pulling up the lane in front of the house. He watched as Nathan sprang out of the car and crossed over to the kitchen door. He wondered if anyone in Comfort Crossing ever used their front doors. Well, Jenny's parents had, and Joseph's parents. Must be a "which side of the tracks you live on" thing.

"Hello, sir." Nathan greeted him when he pushed open the back door.

"Come in. Danielle will be down in a minute."

Abigail came bouncing into the house and over to Nathan.

"Hey, Short Stuff. What's up?"

Abigail smiled at him and held up the kitten in her hands.

"A kitten? Did you pick out a name for it yet?"

Abigail shook her head no.

"Well, you better be picking one out soon. We can't go

around calling it Kitten forever."

Abigail nodded enthusiastically.

Just then, Danielle came downstairs, in a barely better outfit than before. Same short skirt, but at least she had a shirt on over her tank top. Though, he really had no illusions that she wasn't going to peel it off as soon as she got out of his sight.

"You ready to go?" Danielle asked Nathan, obviously ready to escape the unrealistic oppression of her father.

"Sure thing." Nathan turned to Abigail. "See you later, Short Stuff."

"Nathan?" Clay stopped the boy by resting his hand on the boy's arm. "I want her home by eleven."

"Dad." Danielle broke in, shoulders set, all ready for a fight. Most things were a fight with her these days. It was tiring.

"That's cool. I have to have the car back by eleven-thirty, anyway." Nathan cleverly avoided a scene.

"Okay, I'll see you at eleven. Sharp."

Danielle looked like she started to roll her eyes at him, but thought better of it.

"Goodbye, Mrs. Miller."

"You kids be good."

"Drive safely. Wear your seat belts." Clay couldn't help adding.

This time Danielle let out a big sigh of exasperation and led Nathan out the door. The two teens crossed the porch and headed for the car. Clay watched while

Nathan held the door open for Danielle. The kid had manners, he'd say that much for him.

"Clay, I packed a picnic supper for you and Jenny." Greta motioned toward a picnic basket sitting on the counter.

"Mom, you didn't have to do that."

"Well, if I know you—which I do—and you two want to talk, you'll head out by the stream. Thought you'd like a picnic supper to go along with the conversation. Just remember, son, Jenny has had a hard year."

"I know, Mom. Mine hasn't been such a piece of cake either." He sounded whiney even to his own ears. "I'm sorry. Thanks for making the picnic. I appreciate it."

"Kind of reminded me of the old days, when you were in high school." Greta smiled at him. "Now run upstairs and get ready."

"Abigail, you'll be fine here with Grams?" His daughter nodded silently. For a brief, flashing moment, he wished Nathan would come back and make his daughter laugh again.

He climbed the stairs to change clothes after a day of nonstop patients at Doc Baker's. He'd have to hurry or he'd be late picking up Jenny. Then he laughed out loud. How many times in his life had he had that exact thought while he rushed up these very same stairs?

* * * * *

Clay stood at her door, looking good in the early evening light. His eyes held a hint of boyish charm, his smile a hint of playfulness. He was blissfully unaware she was about to rock his world.

"You ready?"

"Sure, just let me grab my handbag." Jenny scooped her bag off the counter. Her house phone rang and she paused, wondering who it might be. "Just a second, Clay." She walked over and snatched the phone off the cradle while Clay stood in the doorway.

She answered the phone and mouthed the words "my mother" to Clay. He nodded.

"Mother? Is everything okay? Is Father okay?" Her mother's voice sounded strained. "Well, do you need me to come over?" Jenny dropped her bag back on the counter. "Okay, I'll stop by tomorrow, then. I'll put a call into Father's doctor in the morning and see what he says. Love you, too." Jenny settled the phone back in the cradle.

"Father is sick. Mother isn't handling it very well. He's always done everything for her."

"I remember."

"Mother talked to the doctor, but she isn't really sure what the doctor wants to do. I'll check with him tomorrow. Father's been sick a long time now."

"I'm sorry. Are you sure you don't want to go by tonight?" Clay didn't look like that was the choice he wanted her to make. She couldn't blame him. Clay knew her father never had liked him, and that was putting it very mildly.

"No, the morning will be fine." There really wasn't anything she could do tonight. Her parents had a nurse who came by twice a day to check on her father. He'd already gone to bed for the evening, anyway. Not much she could do tonight. She dug around in her purse looking for her keys. Why could she never find them?

"So, where are we going?" Jenny had no idea where would be a good place to be alone and try to explain what she'd done.

"Well, Mom made a picnic supper. I thought maybe we'd go out to the stream behind Mom's place. Remember that willow where we always used to hang out? I haven't been there in years. If you want to talk, there aren't a lot of places to go in Comfort Crossing without a lot of prying eyes."

Somehow the stream seemed a fitting place. They had spent hours there in high school. Just the two of them, or sometimes Joseph, Becky Lee, and Izzy would join them. They talked about life and their future, spent hours talking about really nothing at all and splashing in the stream. It was the first place Clay had ever kissed her, the first place he had made love to her. Yes, it seemed like as good a place as any to go talk.

They drove without saying a word. Jenny was too nervous to concentrate on small talk, and Clay seemed comfortable with the silence. He used to say that just being with her was enough. He hadn't ever tried to fill the quiet that sometimes fell between them up with words.

He fiddled with the radio and some soft country music filtered through the speakers. She could hear him hum the tune under his breath. He always used to do that, or break out singing if he really liked the song. She looked over at him. It pulled at her heartstrings. Driving down the back roads, listening to country music with Clay. If only she didn't have to ruin the evening. Didn't have to blow up the lives of so many people.

He pulled into the dirt lane that went past the back of Greta's property. Clay parked the car by the side of the road and came around to help her out. He reached a hand out to help her. She just sat there like a fool, looking at the strong familiar hand.

"Come on, Jenns. I don't bite." He smiled at her.

She took his hand and slid out of the car. He snagged a blanket, and the picnic basket from the back seat. They headed for the stream, just a short walk away. The branches of the bushes crowding the sides of the overgrown path grabbed at them as they pushed closer to the stream. Clay carefully held back the branches for her as they went along the overgrown pathway, a poignant reminder of how long it had been since anyone had been out here.

The stream gurgled a beckoning sound in the background. A breeze picked up and the air cooled slightly as they approached the stream and broke into the opening beside it. The old willow tree swished its branches in the soft breeze. Fireflies danced in the dusky light. Jenny caught her breath at the unexpected magic spell this spot still held over her.

Clay spread out the old blanket, like he had so many times before, and sat down. He reached into the basket and grabbed a bottle, his hands sure and steady as he poured them some sweet tea. He handed her a glass and she reached out to take it from him. Their fingers brushed slightly and she resisted the urge to pull away. She'd probably end up spilling the tea all down her dress. Clay sat down and leaned against the willow tree. The evening had become a strange mix of past and present, the images tangled in her mind, seducing her back to the past.

"You going to sit down, Jenns?"

"What? Oh, sure." She sank down on the soft blanket. The distant sound of thunder rumbled across the evening sky.

"I guess that cool front is coming in."

"Seems like it. At least the breeze has kicked up some." She straightened out her dress and took a sip of sweet tea. Were they going to make inane small talk the whole night? No, she could answer that question. They weren't. She was going to tell him...

"Jenny? Why did you marry Joseph?"

The question caught her by surprise. No, she guessed they weren't going to make small talk at all anymore.

"I— He... Well, he asked me and I said yes."

"But why?"

Why indeed? So many reasons. So many choices. She figured she'd start with the truth. "I was lost without you, Clay. I didn't know which way to turn. Joseph was there for me."

"Did you go out with him while you were dating me?" His eyes flashed steel blue and the corners of his eyes held a hint of insecurity he was unable to hide.

"How could you even ask me that?" Jenny twisted and looked him straight in the eye. Her heart clutched with an ache of hurt. This man still had the power to upset her so easily.

"It was just so quick. You married him so soon."

Jenny knew this was the time, the perfect opening. As if the heavens agreed with her, a bright flash of lightening lit up the distant sky again.

"Clay…"

"Jenny, I've missed you. I know you don't believe it, but it's the truth."

Now that wasn't something she thought she'd ever hear from Clay. It made her ache for what they used to have. What they could have had. She didn't know what to say, so she just simply said, "I've missed you too, Clay."

"I was such a fool." Clay leaned closer to her and brushed her hair away from her face. "I've spent years being angry with you and Joey, but I know it was my fault. I deserted you."

"I did feel deserted, Clay. I didn't know where to turn.

Joseph felt sorry for me, I guess. I felt so alone."

"But you and Joey were happy?"

"We were. We made a life for ourselves. I think he came to love me. I know he loved Nathan. And I—cared —about him deeply. I loved him in my own way."

"I should have been there for you. I should've never let —" Clay broke off his words and tangled his fingers in her hair. He ran his thumb along her jaw line.

The trail of his touch left a burning brand along her jaw. Her breath came quickly now, her traitorous automatic reaction to Clay Miller's touch. She had no power against it. Never had.

Clay ran his hand up her arm. Immediate goose bumps appeared. Her heart began to beat faster. His touch was warm and electrifying, like the distant lightening still illuminating the sky.

He leaned closer and she knew he was going to kiss her. She wanted him to kiss her. She wanted him to want her again, just for this brief moment in time. One last time, before she ruined everything. It was selfish, and she knew it. She wasn't proud of it. But she wanted this man. One last time with him. After all these years of wanting him. Of missing him.

She argued with herself. Selfish. *Pull away. Tell him.* Then she felt his lips close on hers. Warm lips, strong and gentle at the same time. He pulled her into his lap and wrapped his arm around her, moving his hands down her back. Touching her face, sliding his palms down her arms. His touch was everywhere. His kiss was all inclusive. There was no part of her that didn't come alive.

"Jenns." His breath came in a gasp. "I didn't…"

"Shh." She put her finger to his lips. She gave up the battle, knowing she'd regret it later. But now, right now, she needed him to want her. To make love to her. She buried her face in his neck and held on for dear life. She was drowning and no one could save her.

"I've missed you." His soft words were murmured against her neck.

The night sky exploded in lightning and thunder around them as their own private storm raged and they gave in to seventeen years of wanting each other.

Chapter Eight

Jenny felt terrible and wonderful at the same time. Her emotions were at war with each other. She was so happy to be back in Clay's arms. It felt so wonderful to have him want her again, for him to make love to her, but she knew she still had lied to him. Worse yet, she'd made love to him knowing she needed to tell him the truth. She despised herself right now. How could she have been this self-centered? It wasn't fair to Clay.

Time's up. He had to be told the truth. She would just have to take this memory and wrap it around her and hold on to it when Clay's wrath descended upon her. Which she knew it would.

"Clay, we need to talk." It took all her strength to drag herself away from him. She pushed herself off of his chest and sat up, reaching across the blanket to grab her sundress. She held the dress in front of her to cover herself up.

"Come back and lie down next to me. Don't get up yet." Clay's voice was mellow and low, coaxing her.

"I need to talk to you."

"Jenny, don't go feeling guilty or anything. I couldn't take that."

"I have to tell you something."

"Um?" He reached over and touched her face.

She pulled back. "I'm serious. We need to talk." Lightning streaked through the sky, and the thunder rumbled.

"I have a better idea. You come curl up beside me and let me hold you."

His voice pulled at her, coaxed her, taunted her. "Clay..."

A crash of thunder made her decision for her. Thank goodness. Because she was pretty sure she was a weak woman and would have slid right back down beside him and started something up again.

Clay sat up. "Hey, we better get dressed and head for the car. This storm is going to hit any minute." He leveraged himself up and reached for his clothes. Another crack of thunder exploded.

Jenny stood up and slipped the sundress back on. The material felt rough and invasive against her skin. Big drops of rain started to splatter around them.

"Hurry." Clay gathered up the blanket, tucked it in the picnic basket and turned toward Jenny.

Jenny slipped on her sandals. Clay's warm hand

wrapped around hers, and they made a mad dash for the car. The rain let loose with its full blown fury before they could reach safety. Jenny figured the heavens were mocking her for her deceit. She was drenched to the skin when she slipped inside the car. Clay slid in beside her and shook his head. The drops of water flew in all directions and he laughed. A full laugh that filled the car and only showed her what a big mistake she'd made. Huge.

Water dripped from Jenny's hair and slid down her shoulders. Clay reached over with the blanket and wiped her face. He turned her to face away from him and gently toweled her hair with the blanket. She had no will power when it came to this man. None. Jenny relaxed into his touch, more of a massage than anything else. The rain pounded the roof of the car, but she was safe inside with Clay.

He tilted her back against his chest and rubbed his hands up and down her arms. "You cold?"

No, the goose bumps weren't from cold. They were from his touch. "I'm okay."

He shrugged out of his wet shirt and tossed it into the back seat. His chest glistened in the dim light. She so wanted to run her hands along the muscles. Touch him. Heat him up so he'd never forget her touch. She stopped herself. She dredged up the willpower from some unknown recess and clenched her fists in her lap to keep from reaching out to him. The truth. First the truth.

"Clay..."

His beeper went off, a jarring noise through the pounding of the rain on the roof of the car. He checked the number on the pager, then snagged his cell phone from the picnic basket. "No bars, no service. It's Mom. She wouldn't page me unless it was important. I need to get home and see what she needs. Maybe it's the girls, or maybe a patient called the house looking for me since my cell isn't picking up service here."

Jenny nodded. "That's fine. Let's go." She straightened in the seat and clicked on her seatbelt. She'd still tell him tonight. After he found out who needed him and dealt with it. She would not let this night end without Clay knowing the truth about his son.

He put the car in gear and pulled out onto the gravel road. The rain pounded on the roof of the car, unleashing its fury. She shivered, her skin still tingling from Clay's touch, her mind jumping from thought to thought, scared of the confrontation ahead of her tonight. She was embarrassed she'd given into his fiery touches and made love to him tonight with the secret still between them. But, if she'd just admit it, in her heart she was glad she'd had this one last time with Clay. No matter what the cost, no matter what price she had to pay.

* * * * *

A police car sat in front of Greta's house when they pulled up. Clay's pulse quickened. It might just be the police out trying to find him to help a patient, or something else. Jenny clutched at his arm. He snatched his shirt from the back seat and pulled it on. He reached over for Jenny's hand and pulled her out of the car right behind him. He felt her warm hand in his as they raced for the porch. She was there with him, whatever he had to face.

"Mom!" Clay pushed through the kitchen door. He took it in with a glance, Nathan and Danielle sitting quietly at the kitchen table. The sheriff was reaching for a cup of coffee from Greta's hand.

He dropped Jenny's hand and looked over at the table again then at Greta. "What's going on?" His heart still pounded in his chest, but here was his daughter, alive and well.

"Clay, you remember Mark Dawson. He's the sheriff now." Greta reached out a hand to rest on Clay's arm.

"Hey." Clay shook the sheriff's hand. "Is there a problem?" He glanced over at Danielle. His daughter poised on the edge of her chair, staring straight ahead at the wall and avoiding her father all together.

The sheriff turned towards Jenny. "Ma'am." He motioned to the teens at the table. "I caught these two leaving Eddie Fever's. We got called out there for a party that got out of hand. Underage drinking. And one young fool decided to shoot off a shotgun. They're all lucky to be alive. Ms. Bouchard, young Nathan seems to have a knack for being at the wrong place at the wrong time. I know he's had a rough time with Joseph and everything… He's not really in trouble this time, I just wanted to make sure he got home okay, but he insisted we bring Ms. Greta's granddaughter home. I told Joseph I'd look out for him, you know."

"I know, and I appreciate that." Jenny nodded to the sheriff. She crossed over to stand by Nathan. Clay watched her look directly into her son's eyes. "Have you been drinking?"

"No, Mom, honest. We were just leaving because the party got wild. Some kids from Bayou Corner came by. Things were getting out of hand."

Clay watched Jenny closely. There was this mother son connection that zipped between them, and he could tell the exact moment when she believed him. Completely.

Well, he didn't believe the boy. He had no reason to. Nathan had taken his daughter to some wild party, this boy who had been getting into trouble regularly. Clay wasn't as easily snowed as Jenny. He felt the anger well up inside of him, spurred on by the knowledge that Danielle could have been hurt. It took him by surprise how fast the anger over took him. He balled his hands into fists, trying to grab control, but all he could feel was anger and fear. He walked over to Nathan and Nathan rose to his feet. Clay grabbed hold of Nathan's arm and pressed his finger to Nathan's chest. "You took my daughter to a party like that. Are you out of your mind? Have you not a lick of sense in your head?"

"Clay—" Jenny's voice held a note of surprise, laced with a hint of threat to back off.

Nathan looked up in surprise. "Sir, I didn't know…"

"I don't want to hear your excuses." Clay let go of Nathan. "I don't want you anywhere around my daughter. Do you get that?"

"But Dad…" Danielle stood up.

Clay motioned Danielle to be quiet and stared down Nathan. "No. That's it. You may not see Danielle again. You took her to a party where there were *gunshots*. I don't trust you. There are no second chances. She can't be anywhere near you. Do you understand me?" Clay kept his voice low and controlled, but he was seething inside.

He saw Jenny move closer to Nathan and place her arm around his shoulder. *Go ahead. Protect your son. Just like I'm protecting my daughter.* But he didn't say his thoughts out loud.

Clay felt Greta come up behind him. "Son…"

"No, Mom. I can't have him dragging her into trouble here, too." He turned to the Sheriff. "Sheriff, are you pressing charges?"

"Charges? No, I just wanted to make sure they got home okay. There are still a lot of those Bayou Crossing kids hanging around. I owe Joseph… well, anyway, if I had a son like Nathan, I'd want someone to be looking out for him."

The Sheriff looked at Jenny. "I honestly don't think he's

been drinking, Ms. Bouchard. I followed him back here. I wouldn't have let him drive if I thought he'd been drinking." He turned to Nathan. "You do need to be careful on these back roads, Nathan."

"Yes, sir."

"I'll be leaving now. Thanks, ma'am, for the coffee."

"Thank you, sheriff." Greta showed him to the door.

Clay turned to look at his daughter. "You are not to see Nathan again. Do you understand?"

"Dad, you're not being fair. He didn't—"

"Save it." Clay cut her off. *What if something had happened to her? What if she'd been hurt?*

Danielle got up from the table and went to stand by her grandmother. She pulled herself up straight and shot him one of her infamous you'll-never-understand-me looks.

Jenny dropped her arm from Nathan's shoulder. Her wet dress clung to her and he could see her shiver slightly. Clay wasn't sure if it was from cold or from anger. "Come on, Nathan. Let's go home."

Nathan gave Danielle a long look. Almost a look of apology, as if he was sorry he had gotten her in trouble. Danielle nodded to him and made a gesture that clearly said that everything was okay. Clay glared at both of them.

Jenny turned and gave Clay the most hauntingly poignant look he had ever seen. A look full of regret, that slowly changed to barely disguised anger. Well, he couldn't worry about that now, because Jenny needed to keep her son away from his daughter. That was all there was to it. He couldn't chance losing his daughter because of some stupid teenage risk taking. If Jenny couldn't control her son, then he'd just keep Nathan far away from Danielle.

* * * * *

"Give me the keys, Nathan." Jenny crossed the porch. The storm had slowed down to a miserable drizzle.

"Mom, I'm sorry."

"I know."

"I just wanted to get Danielle away from the party. It just started to get out of hand. It was stupid. I should have left sooner. Those kids from the other town came and brought beer. Someone fired a shotgun. I grabbed Danielle and ran for the car."

"I thought you said Eddie's parents were home."

"They were, Mom. We were all out in the barn. I think they're the ones who called the police when the Bayou Corners kids showed up."

Jenny unlocked the car doors and motioned for Nathan to climb in. She turned on the ignition and slowly put the car into reverse. Everything seemed like a big gigantic effort. It scared her senseless to think that someone had a gun at the party. Nathan could have been hurt. She just couldn't bear that.

Nathan sighed. "Danielle's father hates me now."

"Nathan, he doesn't hate you. He's just protecting his

daughter." But Jenny wasn't sure Nathan's assessment wasn't more accurate.

The more Jenny thought about it, the angrier she got. Her son had gotten Danielle out of a bad situation. He'd brought her home safely. He hadn't been drinking, but Clay had practically exploded at Nathan. If she hadn't known Clay so well, and known he would never throw a punch, she would have been afraid for her son. But then, how well did she even know this new Clay? This older Clay. The one who was so furious with her son. His son. Now what was she supposed to do?

"He was really mad. He doesn't think I'm good enough to be a friend of Danielle's."

If Jenny hadn't been so exhausted… if she hadn't been so mad at Clay for thinking Nathan wasn't good enough to be around his daughter… she might have thought it some kind of karmic justice that the roles were reversed now. A Miller thought a Delacroix grandson wasn't good enough for his daughter.

"I wasn't trying to get her in trouble. I was trying to keep us *out* of trouble. The party got out of control so fast. I was busy talking to Danielle and didn't even notice it at first. But Dr. Miller is right. I shouldn't have taken her somewhere like that. I was stupid."

"You weren't stupid, son. Dr. Miller was just upset. He shouldn't have been saying those things to you. Sometimes parents say things when they're upset or think their kids could have been hurt. He was just upset when he heard about the gunshots." She reached over and patted his leg. "Heck, *I'm* upset about that. Someone could have been hurt. *You* could have been hurt."

"Mom, honest, I took Danielle and got out of there as soon as I realized it was out of control."

"Nathan, I believe you. It was just one of those unfortunate things."

"How come you believe me? Danielle says her dad never believes her. He never listens to her."

"I believe you because I know you're telling the truth. I can't answer why Clay doesn't believe Danielle. Maybe she's done things so he has a hard time trusting her."

"Yeah, she got into some trouble, she said. But so did I earlier this year. I'm sorry about that. I've been such a jerk since Dad died."

Jenny smiled at her son. "Yes, you have."

"Ouch." Nathan grinned back at her.

"We've all had a rough time of it. You're a good kid, Nathan. I always figured you'd find your way back. Sometimes it feels good to act out against the fates, doesn't it? I understood that part. I was worried you'd get hurt, or do something that couldn't be undone, and you'd regret it."

Nathan settled back against the seat, quiet for a bit. Jenny agreed Nathan should have left the party earlier, but that didn't mean he wasn't good enough for Clay Miller's daughter. He had chosen to leave and get Danielle out of there when the party got out of hand.

"Danielle doesn't have any other friends here. She's kind of cool for a girl. She's easy to talk to. I never had a friend who was a girl." Her son paused to look at her. She could tell he was deciding whether to go on. He took his little sigh-breath that he always did when he had made up his mind to talk about something he wasn't sure he should say to her. She almost smiled, but refrained.

"I talked to her about Alexa. You know, the one with the twin brother, Zachary."

Jenny smiled to herself. A to Z all in one set of twins.

Nathan continued, unaware she had gone tangential on him for a moment. "Well, I've been wanting to ask Alexa out for like a year. She's cute and smart. But I didn't have the nerve to ask her out. Danielle told me to just go do it. Then she dared me." Nathan smiled then. "I had just started over to Alexa when the party got wild. I went back to Danielle and got her out of there." He turned to look out the window. "I am going to ask Alexa out, though. Danielle was right. I'm being a wuss."

There he was, finally admitting to liking Alexa. She skipped that point and moved onto his friendship with Danielle. "I'm sure Danielle likes having you as a friend too, but we'll have to respect Clay's wishes. I don't agree with his choices, but he's Danielle's father."

"But Mom, it's not fair. She doesn't have anyone else to talk to here."

"Life is not always fair."

"I know that, Mom. Sometimes it's not fair at all."

Nathan turned and looked out the window. "I wish Dad were here."

Jenny looked at her son. The boy-man. Trying so hard to grow up and deal with the punches life had thrown him. She reached out and touched her son's cheek. "I miss him, too."

Chapter Nine

"Mother?" The next morning, Jenny searched her parents' house. Usually her mom was in the front sitting room at this time in the morning. She didn't want to call out very loudly in case her father was still asleep. Though she doubted her mother would hear her through the enormous house that no one had ever mistaken for a home. The house with its tall white pillars playing sentinel out front to the massive oak doors that led into a vast, dark entryway. Her steps echoed on the floor, mocking the cold emptiness around her. She once again wondered, like she had her whole life, how a house could have so many things in it—expensive things, proper things—and still feel so empty.

She went into the kitchen to ask the cook if she'd seen her mother. Cook told her that her mother was out on the back veranda. She found her mother sitting outside, sipping some tea, and staring out at the gardens. The ceiling fan slowly stirred the morning heat, just enough to make it comfortable to sit outside.

"You okay, Mother?" Jenny crossed the veranda and sank into one of the chairs next to her.

"I'm fine, dear. Nice of you to stop by."

"Father any better this morning?"

"I think so. His nurse was getting him up and dressed. I'm sure she'll bring him down shortly."

A cook for their meals. A maid who cleaned. A nurse who took care of her father. The life she came from but never embraced. She had learned to cook and had enjoyed sitting down with Joseph and Nathan while they all talked about their days.

Her mother looked lost these days. Her routine of so many years had been turned upside down. Father no longer went to work each day, hadn't in over a year. Not that they needed the money, but he wasn't a pleasant man to be around when he wasn't kept busy.

"Jennifer." Her father came out on the veranda using a walker. She was sure he hated being dependent on it. He shuffled over to a chair beside them and sat down, shaking off any help from his nurse. "Tell Cook to bring me my coffee." He dismissed his nurse with a nod.

"Haven't seen you in quite a while, Jennifer. Too busy to visit your parents?"

Jenny held back. It was always like this, with some imagined transgression. How she lived her life wrong, or some way she didn't live up to her father's expectations.

So she ignored his question and asked one of her own. "You feeling better, Father?"

"Just great. Can't get myself dressed anymore. Can't walk without that ridiculous walker. Why wouldn't I be fine?"

"I'm sorry, Father."

"What are you sorry about?"

"I just meant…"

"I don't want your pity, Jennifer. But you could bring that boy of yours around more often."

Jenny knew she had been lacking there, but her father was just as hard on Nathan and as critical of him as he was of her. She just couldn't bring herself to subject Nathan to that very often. He seemed to understand and take it in stride, but what mother wanted to put her son through that?

"I'll bring him by soon."

"Hmph." Her father adjusted in his chair and reached out to take his coffee from the cook, who had appeared quietly at his side. No thanks were given. As far as he was concerned, it was Cook's job, no thanks needed.

Jenny smiled at Cook before she headed back inside. Jenny bristled at the way her father lived. The way he treated people. He was a cussed old man, but she loved him because he was her father.

She still remembered the day she figured out she didn't like him though. Nathan had been two years old and her father had made some remark about Nathan being a spoiled rotten child when he had got into the pots and pans in the kitchen and was banging away at his band. Her father had walked in at that very two-year-old moment and criticized Jenny's mothering skills. Criticized her child. In that moment, the realization had come to her that she could still love her father, but not like him much at all. It had been a life changing moment for her.

She resolutely ignored his criticism. "I'll check with the doctor today and see how he thinks you're getting along."

"He's a quack. Doesn't know what he's talking about."

"Well, I'll just see what he says."

Her mother smiled at her, but remained quiet. Her mother was usually quiet when her father was around. That's how the house was. Always.

"Well, I've got to run. I need to go into the school for a bit and get things set up."

"Don't know why you're working, anyway. Joseph should have left you enough money so you didn't have to."

Jenny counted to three. Then to five. "Father, I enjoy teaching."

"Doesn't seem right, him leaving you and you having to go to work."

"I worked before Joseph's death, Father. Ever since Nathan started school."

"Just not right."

Jenny rose up and pressed a kiss on the side of her mother's face. "Call me if you need me," she whispered to her mom.

"Bye, Father."

"Have Cook bring my breakfast."

Her heels clicked on the gleaming wood floors as she crossed the hallway and stopped in the kitchen to nicely ask Cook to bring her father his meal. With quick strides, she escaped the dark oppressiveness of the house she grew up in and in which she had always felt like a stranger.

* * * * *

"Are you crazy? Or just headed for heartache again?" Becky Lee reached across the booth and took Jenny's hand.

"I know. I can't believe it either. I'm just stupid when it comes to Clay Miller."

"He's going to break your heart again."

"No, he's not going to have my heart to break." Jenny took her hand back and sipped her coffee. Magnolia Cafe was almost empty. The cook was at the grill in the back, cooking up the order for the one other customer in the cafe at mid-morning. Becky Lee was the only waitress on duty.

"Clay was so furious at Nathan, like Nathan had done something horribly wrong to his daughter, like he was a bad influence on her."

Becky Lee flashed her genuine, tickled-to-the-bone

smile. "That's kind of poetic justice, now isn't it? A Delacroix not good enough for a Miller."

"I thought the exact same thought last night, driving home with Nathan. He was so hurt. Darn Clay for making him feel that way. I thought he did the right thing, leaving that party. Okay, he could or should have left earlier, at the first sign of trouble. But he did leave. He hadn't been drinking. I'm sure of it."

"Yeah, poor Nathan. He's always been a lousy liar. Ever since he was a little kid, it's just right there on his face."

"Yes, well actually that's a helpful attribute in a child." Jenny smiled at her friend.

"So, what are you going to do now?"

"I need to tell Clay the truth about Nathan. He needs to know it. I can't keep it from him any longer. I'm just afraid of the fallout from telling him. And Nathan. And Joseph's parents."

"So you told me about the run in with Clay and Nathan. Heck, half the town knows about the party at Eddie Fever's last night and that the sheriff was called in. But what happened before all that?"

"We went to the stream."

"You didn't!" Becky Lee rolled her eyes. "Tell me you didn't really."

"We did. Greta had packed a picnic supper. It was so peaceful there, like it used to be when life was simpler. I thought it was as good a place as any to tell him the truth.

So much of our past was there."

"So what stopped you?"

"I got… sidetracked. He said he missed me. *He missed me.* Can you believe that? I never thought I'd hear those words from Clay."

"He always did know how to mess up your mind, Jenny girl."

Jenny wasn't ready to share any other details of their time by the stream, though if anyone in the world would understand it was Becky Lee. She always seemed to understand where Jenny's head and heart were, sometimes better than Jenny did.

"It's like he still holds some kind of spell over me. I'm not amused. Though I think he probably broke the spell last night when he lit into Nathan." Jenny felt her anger rising up again. "Nathan was hurt by it. What kind of man jumps down a kid's throat like that? He's a doctor for Pete's sake."

"He's also a father. He was probably scared for his daughter. I can't believe someone had a gun out there last night." Becky Lee continued rolling up the stack of silverware in front of her. Napkin down, plunk down a knife, fork, and spoon, roll it up in the napkin. "Eddie Fever's father came in this morning. He was in some foul mood. Nathan was right, it was Mr. Fever who called the sheriff. All sorts of not so nice comments about the Bayou Corners kids."

"I can't believe there was a gun there either. This

raising a kid thing is scary enough without throwing in guns."

"So I guess you didn't get a chance to tell Clay the truth then, did you?"

"I was just getting ready to. Then his beeper went off and he rushed back to Greta's. The sheriff was there in the kitchen. Nathan and Danielle were just sitting there at the table." Jenny sighed. "Clay got so ticked off at Nathan. So convinced Nathan isn't good enough for his daughter. Insisting Nathan never see Danielle again. Greta tried to stop him, but Clay was so darned convinced he was right, that Nathan was some kind of horrible influence on Danielle. I just took Nathan and went home."

"So now what are you going to do?" Becky Lee added another napkin roll to the stack on the tray.

"I don't know." Jenny looked out the window. A shot of sunshine bounced off a passing truck. "Oh, I know. I mean, I have to tell him. It just seems like now is a bad time. But I'm not going to use that as an excuse. I'm going to tell him."

"When?"

"Not letting me off the hook, huh, Bec?"

"Well, if you're sure he needs to know, then you're just torturing yourself by prolonging it. And I do think it's time, Jenny. We were young when you got pregnant. He dumped you. Your dad would have killed you. An unwed mother? I shudder to think of what your father would have done. Joseph gave you the perfect way out.

And Joseph was a good guy. He was a great dad to Nathan."

"I know. He was. And we had a good life. I was happy. I think Joseph was, too. He said he was. It just seems like all our reasons when we were young sound so hollow now. I was so sure I was doing the right thing back then. I was afraid of my father. I felt so alone and abandoned. I should have told Clay back then and given him a chance, but I was just a scared kid and I didn't want Clay because of his unbreakable sense of duty. I wanted him to love me and want me. I wanted him to be happy he had a son. But I just couldn't see my life married to a man who married me out of some sense of responsibility."

"I think you really made Joseph happy, too. He went into the marriage knowing everything and still wanting it. He was born to be a father, I think. Well, except for the fact he couldn't have any of his own. It just broke my heart when you guys found out. So, in a way, you gave him his one shot at fatherhood."

Jenny nodded. "He was so good with Nathan. I think Nathan enchanted Joseph from the first day I put him in his arms." She sighed. "But you're right. It's time Clay knows the truth. And Nathan. I'm dreading trying to explain this to Nathan."

"Becky Lee. Order's up," the cook called out from the kitchen.

Becky Lee slid out of the booth with the tray of wrapped silverware and leaned close to Jenny's ear. "Call

Clay up and go see him. Though possibly not down by the stream this time."

* * * * *

Becky Lee watched her friend walk out the door to the cafe and into the blazing heat. She sighed. Jenny just could not resist Clay Miller, no matter how many times he hurt her.

She grabbed the tray of rolled napkins and set it on the counter. Her shift was over soon. She often took the early morning shift, as she'd always been an early riser. Keely, the owner of Magnolia Cafe, would be in soon. Keely's family had owned the cafe for years. Her father had passed on a few years back, and her mother rarely came to the restaurant anymore, so Keely had taken over running the cafe.

Becky Lee was pretty sure that Keely wasn't thrilled to be running the cafe, but she'd made a success of it. It was much more financially successful than when her father had run it.

Becky Lee had started as a waitress at Magnolia Cafe back when she was just a girl in high school, and she still liked working there. It suited her just fine. She liked talking to the townspeople who came into the cafe.

She was lucky that she had inherited a bit of money, enough to buy a small cottage just blocks from the cafe. She didn't have many expenses, she lived simply, and really just liked being a waitress. She was sure that some folk thought it strange, but she was okay with that. She was basically happy with her life.

Unlike her friend, Jenny, who was hopelessly wrapped up in the secrets that had been kept. Not that she blamed Jenny for marrying Joseph to give Nathan a father and a name. Jenny's own father was a cantankerous mean old man. She was pretty sure he would have insisted Jenny give up Nathan and Becky Lee couldn't imagine Jenny's life without him. So, things had worked out. Kind of. It was time for Clay to learn the truth, but Becky Lee sure didn't envy her friend having to tell Clay, then Nathan, then Joseph's parents.

Becky Lee looked up and waved as her last customer left the cafe. She walked over to clear his table. He wasn't a regular. She saw that he had left a ten dollar tip on a seven dollar breakfast. Well, he was welcome to come back any time he wanted.

* * * * *

Clay liked the familiar routine he had fallen into since they had come to Comfort Crossing. Come home from work, talk with Greta in the kitchen while she finished up dinner, and set the table for her. Abigail would come down and sit at the table and listen to them, nodding her answers to the questions they would ask her. Danielle usually waited until the last minute to come downstairs, but they all had a sit down family dinner together. For that, Clay was very grateful to his mom.

Tonight was no exception. Greta was making beans and rice for dinner, a typical southern fare. She'd baked a loaf of bread, and the kitchen was filled with the wonderful scents of bread and spices.

"Could you hand me the salt?" Greta motioned to the shaker sitting on the counter. Clay retrieved it and set it on the stove top near his mom. She gave him the eye when he tried to swipe a taste of the bean mixture.

He grabbed some glasses from the cabinet and filled them with ice. Greta had made a big pitcher of sweet tea. He filled a glass and leaned against the counter.

"Clay, I know you won't want to hear this, but you were pretty rough on Jenny's boy last night."

"He took Danielle to an out of control party."

"That happens around here sometimes. You know that as well as I do. There were parties that turned wild when you went to them, too. Remember when that knife fight broke out after the homecoming game your junior year?"

"Mom, there were *shots* fired."

"I know. But Nathan got Danielle out of there as soon as they realized the party had gotten out of hand."

"I can't risk her being hurt."

"You're not going to lose her, son. You can't protect her from everything."

"Well, she's not going to hang out with Nathan and see what other trouble he can drag her into."

"She hasn't met many people here."

"Well, she can do things with her family while we're here."

"She's a teenager. She likes to hang out with kids her

age."

"Look, I know I was rough on Nathan. I was so scared when I heard about the shotgun." Clay raked his fingers through his hair. "I can't lose her."

"Clay, not everyone leaves you."

"Claire did."

"Yes, she did, and I reckon I'll never understand how a momma can leave her children, much less a man like you. But she did and you have to move on."

"Jenny left me and married my best friend."

"Clay, be honest. You broke up with her. She didn't leave you."

"I know. But it seems I always lose the people I care most about." Clay couldn't decide if he should tell his mom why he broke up with Jenny, but there didn't seem much point now, after all these years. She'd probably feel guilty he did it in part to protect her job.

"Danielle isn't going to leave you, son, unless you push her away. She's just growing up. I'm as worried as you about stupid teen tricks like firing a shotgun at a party. Hope Sheriff Dawson finds the kid who did it and puts the fear of God in him. But Danielle is a good girl."

"I know, Mom."

"Jenny was really mad at you by the time she left last night."

"No kidding. I have this knack of being able to make her angry in no time at all."

"You could call and apologize to Nathan. That would

go a long way. Or, better yet, go over there and apologize in person."

Clay sighed and took another sip of sweet tea. "I'll think about it."

Greta gave him the eye again.

"No, I really will. I'll try to get by tomorrow."

"Why don't you call the girls for dinner?"

Clay crossed to the bottom of the stairs and called upstairs. "Girls, time to eat."

Abigail came bouncing down the stairs and threw herself into his arms. "Hi, sweetpea. Have a good day?"

She nodded at him.

Danielle slowly clumped down the stairs and walked right past him without a word. She slid into her chair in stony silence. Danielle was infamous for her cold shoulder routine. Clay decided to ignore it.

Greta and Clay carried on a conversation through dinner, with Abigail occasionally nodding or shaking her head. Danielle's conversation was limited to "please" and "thank you" when her grandmother asked her if she wanted something. Clay couldn't take it any longer.

"Danielle, how long are you going to keep this up?"

"What?" Danielle asked with false innocence.

"You know what. The cold shoulder. The not talking."

"'Til I'm not mad any longer."

"Until *you're* not mad? You could have been killed! There was a shotgun at the party."

"You were horrible to Nathan. It wasn't his fault. The

party got out of control all of a sudden."

"He took you there. He should have been paying attention to what was going on. It's best if you just stay away from him."

"Dad, that's not fair."

"Danielle, I can't be worrying about you every minute of every day while I'm trying to run Doc Baker's practice. We're only here for another week or so, then we'll get back home right before your school starts. Can't you find something to do that doesn't involve guns?"

Greta flashed him a look. He knew that look. The one where she didn't approve of what he was saying.

Chapter Ten

Jenny pulled in the drive and noticed the garage door was up. Joseph's nineteen-sixty-six mustang was gone. She hadn't been able to part with the car, but thought it was too much of a car for Nathan to drive at his age. She rarely let him drive it, and when she did, he had to ask first.

She hurried up to the house and pushed open the door. The wind had kicked up suddenly and slammed the door shut behind her. Choo Choo looked up, startled. "Sorry, pup."

She dropped her handbag on the counter and reached for the phone. She dialed Nathan's cell, but he'd either turned it off or the phone wasn't picking up a signal. There was no note on the table, which was really unusual. It was an unwritten rule he always had to let her know where he was And he was usually pretty good about it.

She puttered around the kitchen, trying to figure out why he would have left without asking to use the car and without leaving a note. The clock over the kitchen sink ticked away as she picked up the last of the breakfast dishes she hadn't even bothered to load into the dishwasher this morning. She washed off the table and the counter and pushed the button on the dishwasher. Okay, she'd give him one hour before she panicked. It was still kind of early. But he was going to get a stern lecture for worrying her like this.

She went upstairs and slipped into a pair of shorts and a sleeveless top. It had been hot and muggy today after last night's storm. There were brief gusts of wind tonight though, and she wondered if they were supposed to get another storm. She hadn't even checked the weather station this morning. Choo Choo looked up with his big soulful eyes, as if he could tell she was at odds with herself.

Jenny was irritated with Nathan for worrying her like this. She could hardly deal with worrying about Nathan on top of trying to decide when to tell Clay, knowing she had to tell Nathan, too. She'd tell Clay first and see how he reacted.

Then it hit her like the smack of a student's textbook crashing from their desk to the floor. Sudden. Startling. She'd been so worried about Clay being mad. Upset. Furious. But what if he outright rejected Nathan? What if he insisted on a DNA test or something? What if he didn't believe her? Then what would she do?

Chocolate. That's what she needed. She kicked off the sandals she had just put on. It seemed too hot for even wearing sandals. She clipped her hair up to get it off her neck, though it did little to cool her down. She went to the kitchen in search of chocolate and found a frozen chocolate bar in the freezer. Perfect. She grabbed the cordless phone. "Come on, Choo Choo."

She opened the door and the dog followed her out and settled at her feet by the legs of the Adirondack chair. The sweet smell of magnolias drifted across the yard. An occasional burst of wind lifted the hair away from her face. A dog barked in the distance and Choo Choo opened his eyes, but didn't even bother to turn his head. She reached down and patted him on the head. He was such a good dog. She'd never had a pet growing up. Joseph had gotten Choo Choo, a black lab mix who loved them all without fail, when Nathan was about five. She was unfamiliar with the all-out adoration and acceptance a dog could give people. He was getting on in years now, but he still followed her around and looked at her and wagged his tail, as if to let her know he was still there for her.

"Hey, boy. You have any idea where that son of mine is off to?" She scratched the dog behind his ear, watching his one back leg beat a rhythm while she scratched. "Choo Choo, you're the only male in my life who gives me no trouble."

She looked at her watch. It was dark now and a feeling of unease settled firmly down upon her. She wasn't sure if it was knowing she had to talk to Clay, or maybe not knowing where Nathan was, but she just couldn't sit there any longer.

She got up and crossed to the bulletin board by the phone cradle. She punched in the phone number of one of Nathan's friends. By the time she had called his five closest friends, and no one knew where he was, she really began to worry.

She couldn't just sit there. She wrote a note to Nathan and put it on the kitchen table.

Nathan, call me on my cell phone when you get home. I'm out looking for you. Where are you? You are grounded for at least the rest of your life.

Love, Mom.

She grabbed her handbag, keys, and cell phone. "Choo Choo, hold down the fort. I'm going out to look for Nathan." The dog beat his tail against the floor in answer.

Jenny spent an hour driving to all the known haunts. The lake where the kids hung out, a half a dozen friends' houses to see if there were any parties going on. She even drove over to Magnolia Cafe.

She pushed through the front door, and Becky Lee looked up from waiting on a customer to wave to her. Jenny wove her way through the crowd, pausing to talk to one of Nathan's friends sitting at the counter. He hadn't seen Nathan either, and didn't know of any parties going on.

Becky Lee came over. "What's going on? Twice in one day. You okay?"

"I can't find Nathan. He didn't leave a note. I don't know where he is." Jenny knew her voice held an edge of panic. She knew she was overly protective after Joseph's death, but she needed to know where Nathan was at all times. "Has he been by here tonight?"

"No, I haven't seen him."

"I can't think of any place else to look. I checked the lake, drove by his friends' places. No one seems to know of a party going on. Unless, of course, they're hiding it because I'm a dreaded parent."

"Did you call and see if he was with Danielle?"

"Danielle? Clay forbade him to see her."

Becky Lee just raised an eyebrow. "And?"

"You're right. I'm going to call over to Greta's."

She snatched her cell phone out of her purse and dialed Greta's phone number. The number she still had memorized from dialing it a million times when she was in high school.

"Hello?" Clay answered the phone on the third ring.

"Clay? It's Jenny." She heard a long pause.

"What's up?"

"Is Nathan over there with Danielle by any chance? Or out with her?"

"No, of course not. She's upstairs in her room."

"Are you sure?"

"Of course I'm sure. She's been up there ever since dinner. She's not speaking to me."

"I can't find Nathan."

"He's not with Danielle. I'm keeping a tight rein on her right now."

She could almost hear his unspoken words in his disapproving tone of voice. *You should keep a tight hand on your boy, too. He's nothing but trouble.*

"Never mind, then. I'll keep looking."

"Did you try the lake and the cafe?"

"I tried the lake, and I'm at Magnolia Cafe right now."

"I'm sure he'll turn up soon."

"Sorry to bother you." She squeezed out the words through gritted teeth. Clay, with his strict sense of right and wrong. No gray zones. Just the world according to Clay.

"Hope you find him soon."

"Bye." She tapped the end call button on her phone. She was running out of options. So was her son when she caught up with him.

* * * * *

"Who was that?" Greta asked as she entered the kitchen. "I heard the phone ring."

"That was Jenny. She's looking for her son. He went out without telling her where he was going. I told you that boy was trouble."

Greta didn't answer but set down the load of laundry

she was carrying. The basket rested on the edge of the kitchen table.

"I told her Danielle was up in her room."

Greta sank down on a chair and started to fold the clothes in front of her. "Jenny must be worried."

"Well she should learn to control her son better."

"Like I always did with you? Or you do with Danielle? Kids are kids, sometimes. They make stupid choices. We hope they survive them and learn from them."

Clay had the decency to give his mother a properly chastised look. He was being unreasonable. He hadn't been able to control Danielle, with all the trouble she'd been getting into back at home. A parent could only do their best.

"I think I'll go up and tell her to turn down her stereo. It's getting late and Abigail needs to go to sleep."

He climbed the worn wooden stairs and knocked on Danielle's door. When she didn't answer he knocked louder, though how anyone could hear over that stereo was beyond his comprehension. He pushed open the door when she didn't answer after his third knock. He figured her right to privacy was hampered when she played her music so loudly she couldn't hear him knock.

"Danielle?" Clay looked around the room. Empty. *Maybe she was in Abigail's room?* He crossed the hall and peeked in the open doorway of Abigail's room.

"Have you seen Danielle?" Abigail shook her head no.

The bathroom door was open. She wasn't in there. He

decided to check the front porch. He was sure he would have heard her go out, but he went downstairs and checked anyway. Not on the porch. He called out her name. No answer.

"What's wrong?" Greta asked.

"I can't find Danielle."

"She's not in Abigail's room?"

"No, she's not anywhere." He went back upstairs with Greta close behind him. He looked around Danielle's room again.

"She always dumps her things here on the dresser. Her purse is gone," Greta said.

Clay crossed over to the window. "Look, it's open a little bit." He looked out at the porch roof directly below Danielle's window. "You don't think…"

Greta actually grinned at him. "It's not the first time someone snuck out that window."

"I'm going to ground that girl for the rest of her life."

"Why don't you call Jenny back and tell her Danielle is missing? There's a good chance Danielle and Nathan are together."

"I will." He paused. "But I don't want to. I was a pompous, self-righteous jerk when she called, assuring her *my* child would never go against my wishes."

"Call her. Maybe she's still at the cafe."

Greta looked up Magnolia Cafe's phone number. Clay punched in the number. Becky Lee answered the phone.

"Bec. It's Clay. Is Jenny still there?"

"Did you find Nathan? Jenny is worried to death."

"No, but Danielle is missing, too."

"Here's Jenny, I'll put her on the phone."

There was a rustling of noise and voices in the background, then Jenny's voice. "Danielle is gone too?"

"She slipped out the window." He heard the pregnant pause. "Yes, I know. Mom already pointed out to me that's been done before."

"Where do you think they went?"

"I haven't a clue. But I'm going to come swing by the cafe and pick you up. We'll go look together."

"I'm worried. It's not like Nathan to go and not leave me a note."

"Don't worry, Jenns. We'll find them." He paused. "Then I'm going to strangle both of them."

* * * * *

Jenny stood outside the cafe waiting for Clay. She about hit the maximum stress level she could handle. Her emotions were all jangled. She'd had sex with Clay, for Pete's sake, after all these years. She still hadn't told him the truth. Now both their kids were missing and she was sure Clay was going to be furious with Nathan again. Well, he was just going to have to find out he was furious with his own son, because he was going to learn the truth after they found the kids. Tonight. No more stalling.

A group of three cars, filled with teen-aged kids, pulled into the cafe parking lot. They all tumbled out and filtered past her into the restaurant. Clay pulled into the lot and stopped by the front door. He got out and came around to open her car door for her, always the gentleman. Well, except when he lost his temper with Nathan last night.

"Where to first?" Clay pulled out of the lot.

"We could go check out by the lake again. They have to show up somewhere soon."

Clay nodded. They rode in silence. Jenny could feel the air between them crackle with tension. She felt like she was just on the edge of screaming.

"Jenny. I'm sorry about last night."

Jenny caught her breath. Which part was he sorry about? Making love to her? Yelling at Nathan? "Sorry about what?"

He reached over and touched her knee. "I'm not sorry we made love, if that's what you're asking. Not sorry at all."

"It was a stupid thing to do." She saw him bristle at her remark.

"Why was it stupid?"

"Clay, you're here for what, another week or so? You go back home. I stay here. Reliving old memories isn't going to change how our lives turned out. Reliving old memories isn't love. It's just… well, it's just revisiting the past."

"I don't believe that, Jenns. Last night was real."

"Last night was a mistake. I made a mistake. I got carried away in memories. It won't happen again."

Clay took his hand off her knee. The spot where his hand had rested was now achingly empty. She brushed at the spot with her hand. She saw him notice her movement but he didn't say a word.

He drove on in silence, out past the city lights and toward the county lake. Jenny stared at the white line on the road, watching it slip beneath the front of the car as they sped along.

All of a sudden, she felt like she wasn't going to be able to breathe. She briefly wondered if she were having a panic attack.

"You okay? You look pale." Clay finally said something. The fact he looked truly concerned filtered through her haze of panic.

"Something is wrong."

"What? What do you mean? What's wrong? Are you okay?" Clay pulled the car over to the side of the road.

"I… Something… I mean… Something is wrong with Nathan."

"Jenny, you're just worried. You don't know that."

"Yes, I do. Something is wrong. I can feel it."

Just then Clay's pager went off. Clay had told her Doc Baker had made sure Clay had a pager since cell service was so spotty around Comfort Crossing. He snatched it off his belt and looked at the number. "Jenns, sorry. I have to go to the hospital—an emergency."

"I need to look for Nathan!" Jenny could hear the edge of alarm in her voice.

"Okay, we'll go to the hospital. Let me see what's going on. If I have to stay, we'll call Becky Lee or Mom to come get you and help you look. That will work, right?"

"Something is wrong. I feel it."

"Jenny I have to go get this emergency."

"I know. Turn around and go back. I'll go out on my own and keep looking."

"You're not going out on your own."

She fought off a rising panic. "Maybe it's Nathan."

"It's not Nathan. Calm down."

"The emergency. Something is wrong. I can feel it."

"You look like you're going to pass out at any moment. Just let me see what's going on, and we'll get someone to go out with you if I have to stay long."

Jenny's thoughts weren't clear right now. She knew they had to go to the hospital, but the thought of turning around just drove her to the edge. Unless... unless it really was Nathan. If he were the emergency.

"Take some deep breaths. I'm worried about you."

"I'm worried about the kids."

"We'll find them, Jenns. We will."

But would they find them soon enough? Jenny clenched her fists and stared out the window again, watching the white line reel them back closer to town, away from their search... or her bigger fear... reeling them back toward something terrible.

Chapter Eleven

Clay pulled into the parking space reserved for doctors near the emergency room entrance. The county ambulance sat next to the door, its lights flashing. He could see a flurry of activity through the doorway to the emergency entrance. "Come on. Let me find out what's going on and we'll figure out what to do."

Jenny just nodded and slid out of the car. She hurried along beside him, not taking his offered hand. He was worried about her. She was abnormally pale, and her breathing was shallow, near the edge of a full blown anxiety attack, if he guessed correctly.

"It's okay." He hoped his low, controlled voice would soothe her and give her some measure of comfort. He was worried about Danielle, too. He never knew what stunt she was going to pull. He scrubbed his hand over his face.

Clay crossed over to the desk in the emergency room.

He could sense, rather than feel, Jenny close at his side. "Dr. Miller." Clay interrupted the blonde nurse at the desk. "I was paged for an emergency."

"Miller?" The nurse looked at the computer screen. "We have a Danielle Miller in room three and—"

Clay didn't even wait to hear the end of whatever the girl was saying. Sheer steely fear speared through him. He sped down the hallway towards room three, berating Jenny's boy for once again dragging his daughter into danger. His heart pounded and he said all the prayers and bribes he could think of in the time it took to go the sixty feet or so.

"Danielle?" He pushed through the door and looked at his daughter sitting on the edge of the bed, covered with blood. His pulse drummed in his ears.

"Daddy." Danielle burst into tears. Her hair was matted and she had blood on her bare legs. A nurse stood beside her bed.

"Are you okay?" Clay crossed the distance to the bed in two strides, quickly doing an assessment of his daughter. He didn't know where all the blood was coming from. "Where are you hurt?" He turned to the nurse. "Where's the doctor?"

He heard a gasp from across the room and turned to see Jenny standing in the doorway. He was momentarily torn between his daughter and Jenny. Jenny looked like she was going to faint dead away, and he couldn't figure out where all the blood on his daughter was coming from.

"Daddy, she's going to faint."

Clay rushed over to Jenny and wrapped an arm around her. He motioned to the nurse to move and he half carried Jenny over to the bed beside Danielle.

"Jenns, sit tight. Put you head down between your knees."

"Nathan." Her voice was a whisper. "Where is Nathan?"

"Danielle, where are you hurt? Was Nathan with you? Where is he?" Clay fired off his questions in rapid succession.

His daughter began to sob. "I'm okay. I am. Nathan…"

"What? What about Nathan?" Jenny pushed up and tried to stand.

"Don't move." Clay commanded.

Sheriff Dawson appeared in the doorway. "They said you were here, Ms. Bouchard. I'm sorry. We sent the ambulance to the accident as soon as we got the call."

"Nathan. Where is Nathan?"

"He's with the doctor across the hall. It's bad, ma'am."

* * * * *

Jenny pushed off the bed. Steady now, like she had drawn every ounce of reserve she had. She was there for her son. No time for any of this fainting nonsense.

Jenny took a deep breath and steeled herself for whatever she may have to face. The sheriff walked with her across the hallway and pushed the door open for her.

She stood in the doorway for a moment, taking in the scene before her. Nathan, so very pale, lying on the bed. A monitor beeped quietly beside him. A pile of his clothes sat on a chair beside the bed, covered in blood. Torn to shreds. There was only one shoe. Where was his other shoe?

A white coated man looked up as she made herself enter the room. She crossed over to the opposite side of the bed.

"You Nathan's mom?"

Jenny just nodded, unsure if her voice would work.

"Your son hasn't regained consciousness, and we're worried about that. We won't know the full extent of any head injuries until he's awake. We ran some tests. He's going to need surgery."

Jenny struggled to focus on the doctor's words. She reached out and covered Nathan's hand. It was cold and motionless. She squeezed it, trying to will him some of her strength.

"He has some broken ribs and a bad break to his ankle. We'll need a pin put in it. We're concerned about internal bleeding, but not all the tests results are back yet."

"He's going to be okay though, right?" She heard her voice come out soft, tinged with a quaver by the end of the question.

"We're still running tests."

The doctor wouldn't commit to anything. She was

more worried about what he wasn't saying. She reached down and gently touched her son's face. "Nathan, sweetheart, can you hear me? It's Mom. I'm right here. You're going to be just fine." If her words could only make it so, if they could only convince her, as well as convince Nathan. And, while they were at it, the words could convince the efficient but detached doctor standing on the other side of the bed.

She hated this hospital. The smell. The ugly grey tile. She'd spent so much time here in the last few months of Joseph's life. In the end, it had claimed him. It was irrational to blame the hospital, but she did. She refused to let it take another person away from her. She leaned down and whispered in her son's ear. "Fight this. Come back to me. Everything will be okay, I promise. Have I ever lied to you?"

Then it struck her. Yes, she had. She'd lied about who his father was. And his father needed to be told the truth right now. He had a right to know his son was here, fighting for his life. She was going to go find him and tell him the truth. Tonight.

"Ma'am? You need to fill out some paperwork for us and authorize the surgery. They have it for you at the desk down the hall." The doctor paused, checked the beeping machine thing, and looked at the chart in his hand.

"You won't take him before I get back?" She didn't want to leave him.

"They are getting the operating room ready. You can see him before we take him up."

She almost thought she saw compassion in the young doctor's eyes, but he was quick to cover it up, if that was indeed what she saw.

"I'll be right back, sweetheart." She squeezed Nathan's hand again. She reluctantly left his side and crossed into the hallway. Clay and the sheriff stood right outside in the hall, halfway between Nathan and Danielle's rooms.

She heard Sheriff Dawson's voice. "I found an open bottle of scotch in the car."

"He was drinking and driving?"

"It looks that way."

"I told him to stay away from my daughter. Now this. Drinking and driving."

She could tell the moment he noticed her standing there. He spun around and his eyes flashed with unconcealed anger. "Did you hear that? Your son was drinking and driving. He could have killed my daughter. Can't you control your own son? I swear, if Danielle isn't perfectly fine I'm pressing charges. Heck, I'm pressing charges anyway. How stupid can he be? And I told him not to see her! He did anyway." Clay's voice was low and dangerous, with a barely reined in modicum of control.

Jenny took a step back in the onslaught of Clay's rage. His eyes were a cold icy blue. She couldn't handle this now. Not now.

"Take it easy, Dr. Miller." The sheriff took a step closer

to Jenny.

"Easy? You think I should be easy on a kid who chose to drink and drive? You should have hauled him in the first time he got into trouble. Giving him a break because he was Joey's kid? That was wrong. He obviously has no sense. Stupid. Stupid. I can't believe he'd do this to my daughter."

Jenny reeled from the attack. She wasn't even going to point out Danielle had obviously snuck out to meet Nathan, though she just couldn't believe Nathan would drink and drive. Not now. She had thought he was getting his footing again, making better choices, avoiding the fast drinking crowd. She was obviously wrong, but she didn't need Clay hammering on about what a terrible person Nathan was, and what an awful parent she was.

She looked at this man she no longer knew. "At least your daughter isn't headed for the OR. The doctors don't know…" She took a deep breath, her heart aching with pain. "I'm sorry Danielle is hurt. I am. I hope she'll be okay. But don't take your anger out on me tonight. Or Nathan. My son is fighting for his life. A head injury. Internal injuries. They don't know…"

She saw a brief flash of something cross Clay's face. Maybe empathy, maybe remorse. But the fear, *that* she could recognize, the raw parental fear of something happening to their child.

She saw Greta standing a few feet away. "Clay, that's enough."

"Mom?"

"The hospital called the house looking for you. I called Becky Lee to stay with Abigail. I wanted to leave her with someone she knew. I just got here. Are the kids all right?"

"They are still checking out Danielle. She needs some stitches, but they think she'll be okay."

Greta walked past her son, and Jenny felt the woman's warm touch on her arm. "How is Nathan?"

Jenny fought back the tears. "He's unconscious. They aren't sure why. They are still running tests. He needs surgery. I have paperwork to fill out." Her random thoughts came tumbling out.

Greta put her arm around Jenny. "Come on. I'll go with you." She turned to Clay. "Tell Danielle I'll be in to see her in a few minutes." Jenny saw Greta give her son one of those Mom-is-so-disappointed-in-you looks. Who knew a mom could still effectively nail a grown son with that look?

"Jenny—" Clay started to talk.

"Just leave me alone." Jenny dismissed him with a sweep of her hand. "And leave Nathan alone. Don't go anywhere near him."

Greta waited with Jenny while she filled out the papers. Jenny stared at the paperwork trying to remember her phone number. And Nathan's birthday. She couldn't remember Nathan's birthday. Greta took the papers from her. "Here, sign here. Give me your insurance card." Greta handed the papers back to the lady at the front desk. "Take a copy of her card, you have her signature, and Nathan should be in your system already. Get the rest of the information from there."

Jenny was so glad Greta took charge. She felt the woman's hand on her sleeve and looked down. Greta had strong, worn hands. They looked like they were capable of anything. They were wrinkled and bent, but firm. She focused on those hands while she let Greta lead her back to Nathan's room. "I'm going to pop in and check on Danielle, then I'll sit with you while Nathan is in surgery, okay?"

Jenny shot her a grateful look. She didn't think she could bear sitting there alone. Waiting. In this horrible hospital. She thought about calling Joseph's parents, but it was late, they would be asleep. She'd call them in the morning, after the surgery, when she knew more. She knew they'd be here in a heartbeat to sit with her, but there wasn't anything they could really do tonight. It would be hard for them to sit here in the hospital again, waiting for doctors to come out and tell them what was going on. No, she'd spare them that, at least until morning.

Jenny entered Nathan's room. A nurse was adjusting a line going into his arm. "We're just about to take him to the OR."

Jenny looked at her son. So pale. So still. When had her little boy turned into this young man? It seemed so easy to keep them safe when they were little, To hold their hand and make sure they didn't run into the street. Warn them about strangers. Pop them in bed, safe and sound, at night. Sure, little kids might be more physically exhausting to raise, but teenagers were a never ending emotional roller coaster. How could Nathan have been drinking and driving? Why would he have done that? And why was he out with Danielle, after Clay had made such a huge deal over not seeing her?

She placed the back of her hand against his cheek. "You have to be strong, Nathan. The doctors are going to fix you all up. You're going to be just fine."

Her son just lay there on the bed, pale, with his eyes closed. She stared at the faint rise and fall of his chest, listened to the quiet beep of the monitor. So pale, just how Joseph had looked in this same horrid hospital.

An orderly dressed in blue scrubs came in. "It's time for me to take him to the OR."

Jenny bent over and kissed Nathan's cheek. "I'll be here. Everything will be just fine. I'll be waiting for you. I love you, son."

"I love you," she whispered again as the orderly wheeled her son away.

Chapter Twelve

Greta came over to where Jenny was sitting in the waiting room. She pressed a cup of coffee into Jenny's hands. Jenny stared down at the cup, barely aware she was holding it.

"Drink some. It's going to be a long night."

Jenny dutifully obeyed, though the coffee held no flavor. She couldn't taste. She was suddenly overwhelmed by the sterile smell of the hospital, the quiet voices of the nurses at a nearby desk, the flashing lights on a board behind them, the muffled sound of someone's footsteps in the hallway.

Greta's strong presence beside her reassured her. "They'll do everything they can for him. Kids are strong. He's a fighter."

The tears slid down Jenny cheeks in hot trails of burning remorse and fear. For the choices she made and the twist of fate dragging her back here to this hospital.

And the worse thought of all, that the fates might punish her and take away her Nathan. She couldn't bear to lose him.

"You should probably tell Clay, you know."

"Tell him?" Jenny looked at Greta blankly.

"About Nathan."

"He was there in the hall. He knows Nathan is in surgery."

"That's not what I mean. You should tell him the truth."

Jenny could see it in Greta's eyes. She knew. She knew Nathan was her grandson, that Clay had a son. Greta put her arms around Jenny. "It's okay, dear."

Jenny was overcome with relief that someone else shared her secret right that very moment. That someone else wanted Nathan to pull through as much as she did. That someone, Nathan's grandmother, was sharing this time with her, worrying with her and being strong for her.

"How did you know?"

"The other day, when I saw Nathan standing next to Clay, I knew he was a part of me. I could sense it. And he has his daddy's eyes. It suddenly all made more sense. Why you married Joseph so quickly, right after Clay had broken up with you."

"I know I have to tell Clay now. I'm not a scared, pregnant teen, anymore. I tried to tell Clay this week. I did. But he got so furious with Nathan the other night. He acted like Nathan wasn't good enough for Danielle. Then tonight... Tonight he was beyond furious. He let loose all his anger against my son, while Nathan lay defenseless in his bed." Jenny paused and looked at the kind woman beside her, the woman who hadn't chastised her, or yelled at her. She was just there for her. There for Nathan. "Greta, I'm so sorry..."

"It's okay. We'll work it all out."

The tears started again, slowly rolling down her face. Jenny swiped them away with the back of her hand and dug in her handbag, searching in vain for a tissue. "I just can't believe Nathan would drink and drive. I thought he was doing better, making better choices. He's been reeling since Joseph's death, but I thought his days of acting out were behind him."

"Kids sometimes make bad choices. You still love them, hope they learn from their mistakes, and move on." Greta handed her a tissue. "You should tell Clay the truth. He'll be there for Nathan. He deserves that chance."

"Oh, Greta, I know he does. I just can't bear his anger right now. I'm not strong enough to deal with it tonight." She sighed, knowing that somehow she was going to have to find the strength to tell him.

Tonight.

Now.

"Maybe if I tell him tonight, he can focus that anger on me, instead of Nathan. I just don't know the words to say.

How to tell him. How to explain. You're probably wondering, too. How it happened. Why I did it."

Greta squeezed her hand. "There will be plenty of time for you to explain to me. You go find Clay and tell him. He'll want to be there for his son. You'll find the words."

Jenny set down the cup of coffee and got up. Greta looked at her encouragingly. "You'll come get me if the doctor comes out?"

"I sure will, dear."

"I'll go find Clay. He's probably down by Danielle's room."

Now the moment was upon her, the moment she'd been avoiding and dreading for seventeen years, she was surprised at her calm. In the scheme of things, Clay's anger at her didn't seem to matter that much. All she cared about was Nathan. Nathan must live.

She walked toward Danielle's room and found Clay standing in the hall. He watched her approach, his steel blue eyes still filled with anger.

"The doctor is examining Danielle one more time. I'm waiting out here. She was uncomfortable with me in the room."

"Is she going to be okay?"

"It looks like it. Banged up. A few stitches. Not that it lets your son off the hook." Clay's eyes held a hard cold anger.

"I need to talk to you for a minute." Jenny stood in front of him, no longer caring about Clay's anger, hardening her heart against it.

"If you're coming here to make excuses for your son, save it. He's lucky he didn't kill Danielle."

"It's not that. He made a poor choice drinking and driving. I'll deal with that when he's better. But I still love him, Clay, no matter what he does." Jenny glanced down the hall and saw an empty waiting room. "Please, will you go down there and let me talk to you for a minute?" She motioned down the hall.

"I'm not sure we have anything to say to each other."

She was tempted to say *fine then, you self-righteous jerk*, but she didn't. "I just need a minute."

Clay nodded and led the way to the waiting room. "Okay. What is it?"

The calm she had managed walking down the hall faded in a wave of almost terror-like fear. Her heart beat in a riotous rhythm, mocking her, urging her on. Jenny looked at Clay, searching for words, knowing he was soon going to unleash all his anger and frustrations and fears of the night on her. He stood there in the dim light. A man afraid for his daughter. Thankful she was alive and basically unharmed. Mad at the boy who had caused it.

"Clay, I don't know how to tell you this. But you need to hear it." The blood rushed through her. She balled her fists at her side, willing herself not to turn and run.

"Just say it. I need to get back to Danielle."

"Clay... Nathan..." Jenny took a deep breath and

stared at a spot on the wall just past Clay's shoulders. Then she knew she had to look him in the eyes when she told him. She looked deep into the depths of those steely blue eyes. "Nathan is your son."

Clay took a step back. She heard him catch his breath. She watched his eyes as they searched her face, burning into her, questioning, his eyes first wide with shock, then narrowing with suspicion.

"What do you mean, he's my son? He's Joey's." Clay's voice was tight and controlled.

She forced herself not to step back. "No, he's yours. I was pregnant when I married Joseph." The ball in her stomach twisted. She wasn't controlled, not at all. She was suddenly scared to death.

"You tricked Joey? You are heartless." He took a step toward her. "How could you do that to him? To me?"

Jenny bristled at the attack, knew it was no less than she deserved and fought for any scrap of courage she could grasp on to. "No, Joseph knew the truth."

"He did?" Clay's eyes narrowed.

"I told him before he asked me to marry him."

"Why didn't you tell me?" His jaw was clenched and his words came out in a staccato beat.

Her words welled up in her throat and she beat down the urge to sob out of control. "I tried to. I went to Tulane to tell you, and you broke up with me, said you wanted your freedom."

"I had a right to know."

"You did. I'm sorry. I was so scared. I was just a kid myself. And I didn't want you to marry me because of a sense of duty." She tried desperately to keep hold of a tiny thread of control.

"So you married Joseph?"

"He said he'd give my son a name."

"He should've had my name." Clay's face hardened with a barely perceivable twitch at the corner of his eye. "How could you keep this a secret all these years?" He took another step towards her. "How could you do that?"

Jenny held her ground, trembling inside, but forcing herself to remain strong. "The plan was to divorce after Nathan was born, but Joseph fell totally in love with Nathan from the first moment he held him. We slipped into this comfortable routine and, before we realized what had happened, we'd become a family."

"And you thought I had no right to know Nathan was my son?"

"Clay, you didn't want anything to do with me." She could hear the pent up pain in her voice, from years of dealing with his rejection.

"That's no excuse. I had a right to know."

"Back then, I thought it was the only way. I was just a scared kid. My father, I was so afraid of what he would do. I was sure he'd make me give the baby away. I just couldn't do that, but I wasn't strong enough to stand up to my father. Joseph's solution seemed my only way out." Her voice was quiet and sad, even to her ears.

"I don't know how you could have done this to me. All these years..."

"Before he died, Joseph made me promise to tell you the truth. Then Nathan started acting out, trying to deal with the loss of his dad—"

Clay interrupted her. "Actually, he lost his dad before he was born, thanks to you."

His words were like sleet pelting down on her. "I needed to give Nathan some time to adjust to his dad's—to Joseph's—death."

Jenny took a few steps away and turned to look out the window, a moment to catch her breath. She couldn't justify it, she could only explain why she had made her decision. How she had felt at the time. She turned back to Clay. "I've been trying to tell you all this week. I started to tell you the night we made... the night at the stream. But then you got paged and we went to Greta's. You were so furious with Nathan, telling him never to see your daughter again, like he wasn't good enough for her. I just wanted to protect him from your anger."

"And all these excuses make it all right? Keeping my son from me all these years?"

"No, they don't make it okay. It's just how it happened and I made stupid teenage choices. Like Nathan did tonight." Jenny reached out to touch Clay, but he jerked away from her. "I'm so sorry. If I had it to do over again, I would have done it differently. Maybe. At the time, I thought I had no choices and Joseph swept in and rescued me. I should have told you, even though you wanted nothing to do with me. I should've given you a choice about wanting your son or not. I know that now."

"Of course I would've wanted my son. You took that choice away from me."

"I know, and there's nothing I can do to change that now. I'm so sorry." The look in his eyes cut through to her heart. The look of anger, but also the look of pain of all he had lost out on in Nathan's life.

"Sorry doesn't cut it, Jenny." He hammered out his words.

"I know that, too. But I wanted you to know the truth now."

"Nathan has no idea?"

"No. But I'll tell him. Give me time to let him get better first. Please, Clay." She panicked now, knowing the whole situation was no longer under her control and her control only. Clay didn't know Nathan. Didn't know what was best for him.

"I don't owe you a thing."

His icy words struck fear in her. What if Clay told Nathan before she had a chance to explain it to him? "Clay, please..."

"Unlike you, I'll try to do what's best for my son. I'll give him time to recover before his world is torn apart— by *you*. You remember it's *you* destroying everything he's thought was a reality in his life. But he will know the truth."

"Clay Miller, every choice I've made regarding Nathan, I've made trying to do what's best for him, wanting him to have a dad who wanted him, saving him from the wrath of my father if I'd been an unwed mother, keeping him from being a topic of gossip in town. Not telling him this last year while he was still reeling from his—from Joseph's death. I always try to do what's best for him. He's my whole world." She was fueled by her own anger now, too exhausted to hold back, too worried the whole conversation was in vain, because Nathan might not make it through the night.

"So you go ahead and be mad at me. You blame me for keeping him a secret. But you just remember, you deserted me when I needed you most. I went there to tell you the truth. You wanted your freedom. You understand this, Clay Miller, I did what I thought was best for Nathan at the time."

Before he could answer, Danielle came out in the hallway. "Daddy?"

Clay turned towards his daughter. Jenny, knowing Clay so well, could tell he was unsteady on his feet, struggling to process the night's events.

Danielle cautiously walked down the hallway as if afraid of how her father would react. "The doctor said I could go home if you sign some papers. But I don't want to. I want to wait and find out if Nathan is okay."

* * * * *

Clay leaned against the doorway, searching for support.

His world was tilting out of control. "Danielle, you need to go home."

"I'm not leaving, Dad. I mean it."

"You're going home." He felt Jenny come up behind him and moved away from her.

"Dad, please. I need to stay. It's all my fault."

"How is this your fault, except for you sneaking out to meet Nathan?"

The doctor came out in the hall and interrupted them. "If you sign her out, she's ready to leave. She's going to be sore. I wrote her a script for pain pills if she needs them."

"Thanks." Clay turned back toward his daughter, standing there, looking so young and so frightened.

"Please, Daddy. I'll go sit in the waiting room. Please let me stay." He was so darn glad she was alive he couldn't bear to refuse her anything right now.

Clay was suddenly tired. Bone weary tired. He nodded to his daughter, and watched as Jenny walked past him, put her arm around Danielle's waist, and slowly walked down the hallway with Danielle leaning against her. He'd sign Danielle's release form and catch up with them in the waiting room, where he would sit and wait for news on his son. His *son*. He kept saying the phrase over and over in his mind. He shook his head. A boy he'd never known he'd had. How could Jenny have kept this from him? Now what if something happened to Nathan before he even got a chance to know him?

He stared down the hall, unable to convince his legs to

walk. He wanted to rail at the fates. He'd lost so much, all because of a stupid decision to allow himself to be threatened by Jenny's father all those years ago. It had set them on the path which led to this, waiting for news on Nathan.

He should go snag Nathan's chart and see what it said about his injuries, then he'd go wait in the waiting room with Nathan's mom, Nathan's grandmother, and Nathan's sister. Nathan. His son.

He scrubbed his hands over his face, trying to clear his thoughts. He had a son.

Chapter Thirteen

Greta sat in the waiting room, feeling the tension crackle between Clay and Jenny. She could see her son kept a tight hold on his anger, his blue eyes steely cold like they always were when he was upset.

She wished she could fix things for both of them, but it was something they would have to figure out on their own. She wasn't sure her son had it in him to forgive Jenny, but she hoped he did.

Jenny's father was a scary man, especially to a scared, unwed pregnant girl. Greta could see why Jenny had married Joseph when Clay had broken up with her. That whole breaking up thing hadn't seemed right to her – not then, not now. She'd swear that Clay had been madly in love with Jenny. That nonsense about wanting his freedom in college? She didn't believe that for a minute.

She'd bet anything that Clay was still in love with Jenny, even though he wouldn't admit it. Of course, the

Nathan thing had really thrown him a curve. Who knew how long it would take Clay to sort through that.

She'd been sure Nathan was Clay's son the first time she saw them standing side by side this summer. She had marveled that she hadn't figured it out sooner. Nathan looked so like Clay had when he was a boy.

She had a feeling that Nathan was going to be all right. She could feel it in her bones, and her bones rarely lied to her. She couldn't wait to get to know him better. A grandson. That suited her just fine.

She just hoped that, given time, her stubborn son, who always saw things in black and white, would be able to forgive Jenny. She hadn't seen things as strictly black and white for years. There was always that gray zone, the one where a person had to choose between two things, neither of them being something they wanted to do. She knew that first hand. Sometimes a person just had to pick one and live with the consequences.

* * * * *

Clay watched his daughter sleep on the couch in the waiting room. Her blonde hair tangled around her face, framing it in a jumbled web of curls. She looked so peaceful there, younger than her years. He could see the tracks on her face from her tears. How he wanted to wrap her up and protect her. Instead, he crossed to the nurses' station and asked for a blanket. He slowly draped it over his daughter and tucked it in, careful not to wake her.

He could feel Jenny watching him. He glanced over to

where she sat, next to his mom. He should say something to her. But what? He was past angry now. He'd hit the stage of exhaustion, from worrying about Danielle and now from worrying he'd never get a chance with the son he'd never known. Jenny had taken that from him, any chance to be a father to Nathan. Joey had hidden it from him, too. The two people he thought he'd known the best had lied to him. For years. He'd missed so much. He'd missed when Nathan cut his first tooth, took his first step, played his first little league game. He'd missed everything. He'd even missed those endless nights of walking back and forth with a sick baby, trying desperately to comfort him. Greta had missed all this, too. He turned to look at his mom, engrossed in a crossword puzzle. It had all started that fateful day Jenny's father had told him to break up with Jenny or else. He wanted to feel hatred towards the man, but the man was dying, punishment enough for his sins.

But how could Jenny have kept this from him? Why hadn't she trusted him enough to tell him the truth? And how could Joey? Though Clay felt vaguely guilty for holding anger towards a dead man. Joey. His friend, who had protected Jenny from her father's wrath by marrying her.

Clay felt his hand clench. So much anger flowed through him. He didn't understand how, even if Jenny was scared back then when she was a kid, she could have kept it a secret all these years. He'd never be able to forgive her.

It struck him, too, that she had made love to him just last night. It seemed like an eternity ago, but she'd slept with him, knowing she was keeping this secret. How could she've done that? He felt his anger start to swell again, and resolutely pushed it back. There wasn't time for that now. He must focus on Nathan.

He got up and went to ask at the nurses' station if they knew anything. No news. He paced the hall outside the waiting room, unable to sit still. What if? He pushed the thought away. The what-if game was useless. Nathan was going to get better. He was going to have a chance to get to know his son. They'd work something out. Nathan could come visit him, and he would come visit Nathan. Maybe Nathan would want to come live with him for a while...

Clay saw the doctor come down the hallway and head toward the waiting room. He stopped him halfway down the hall. "How is Nathan?"

"Are you his doctor?"

Clay looked at him. "No, not officially."

"I'll need to speak to his mother directly, then."

Darn the new privacy laws. Nathan was his son! But, of course, no one knew that. The doctor had to follow protocol. But if it wasn't piercingly clear before how left out of Nathan's life he was, it was struck home by the doctor's dismissal of any right he had to information regarding his son. Clay followed the doctor to the waiting room.

"Mrs. Bouchard?"

"Yes?" Jenny stood up and walked eagerly over to the doctor. Greta set down the crossword puzzle, and Danielle stirred on the couch.

"Your son came through surgery well. We set his ankle. From the test results, it doesn't look like there's any internal bleeding. We're still concerned about his head injury, but we'll reassess that when he regains consciousness."

"So he'll be okay?"

"We still need time, but it's looking better. Like I said, though, we'll know more when he wakes up."

Clay could see the look of relief on Jenny's face, a loosening of the absolute fear that had held its death grip on her throughout the night. He heard her drag in a deep breath of air. She shoved her hair back from her face.

"Thank you. May I see him now?"

"He's in recovery. They'll bring him up to his room soon. Check at the desk to see what room he's been assigned. You can wait for him there."

Clay turned to Jenny and shot her a commanding look. "Give the doctor permission to talk to me regarding Nathan's condition."

Jenny looked at him. "Yes, go ahead and talk doctor-talk with Clay. Anything he wants to know."

* * * * *

Jenny watched Clay and the doctor leave the room. They

stood at the nurses' desk, talking quietly. Clay nodded a few times, stopped the doctor and asked questions. Nodded again. She only hoped the nodding was good.

She felt a surge of overwhelming hope for the first time all evening. Nathan had come through the surgery. There was no internal bleeding. Now he just needed to wake up and prove the head injury wasn't serious.

"You okay, dear?" Greta stood beside her.

"I'll be better when I see Nathan. When he wakes up."

"How about I find out what room he will be in? You can go up there and wait for him."

Jenny nodded. "Thank you for all your help tonight. For being here with me." What would she have done tonight without Greta? The woman had been a rock. Silent. Strong. And so very kind and forgiving to her.

"It was no problem. Do you want me to stay with you in the room? Are you going to be okay waiting with Clay?"

"Clay? Oh, I guess he'll wait up there too, won't he?" Jenny reached up and rubbed her shoulder. Tired. Old. "I doubt if he'll even acknowledge I exist. I'll be okay. He's just very angry with me right now. I can't say I blame him. He has every right to be."

"He'll find a way to deal with it," Greta promised.

"I'm just really too tired and worried to handle his anger right now."

"You two will find a way to deal with all of this. Give it time."

"I hope so." Jenny looked over at Danielle, peacefully sleeping on the couch. "There are so many people left to tell. Nathan, Joseph's parents, Danielle, Abigail." And her own parents. She was going to disappoint her father once again. It was probably no less than he ever expected of her, always thinking she made the wrong choices and did the wrong thing. Always disappointing him in the end and he never let her forget it.

"You worry about all those people later. You just concentrate on getting Nathan all better. We'll deal with the rest of the world after that."

"You are being so kind to me. I can't figure out why you aren't mad at me. I took your grandson away from you. You didn't get to know him and watch him grow up."

"I made some really foolish decisions of my own when I was a young girl. I regret them now but I've learned to live with the consequences. That's all a person can do." Greta smiled at her. "I'm glad the truth is out now. He's a fine boy. He'll come to grips with the truth, too. Just give him time."

"I hope so. I'm afraid it's just going to be one shock too many for him. I'm afraid he'll turn away from me. I can't bear it... He's going to feel like he's losing Joseph all over again." Her heart ached for the pain she knew her son would feel.

"You'll help him through it."

"I have so many regrets…"

"We all have them. It's what you do to get through them and survive that counts."

"Thanks, Greta." This woman accepted her without question. So kind to her tonight. So strong. A rush of relief flowed through her. This remarkable woman knew the truth and she would be a wonderful grandmother to Nathan.

Danielle stirred and opened her eyes. She pushed up slowly and reached a hand up to the bandage on her head. "Is Nathan out of surgery?"

"He is, sweetie." Jenny answered.

"Is he going to be all right?" She started to stand.

"Don't get up. Sit there for a minute." Jenny stopped her. "He came through surgery fine. They're just waiting for him to wake up."

"Can I see him?"

"I think it's best if you go home with your grandmother. Nathan is going to be sleeping for a long time. Why don't you go home and get some rest, then come and visit him tomorrow when he's awake?"

"Grams, can I stay? Please?

"Jenny is right. Nathan is going to be asleep. Let's get you home and into bed. I'll bring you back tomorrow. Okay?" Greta crossed over and helped Danielle stand up. "Let's find your father and tell him I'm taking you home."

Danielle seemed too tired to argue. She walked out the door with her grandmother's arm wrapped tightly around her.

* * * * *

Jenny sat in the sterile vinyl chair waiting for Nathan to be moved to the room. Clay stood staring out the window, saying nothing. The set of his shoulders proved he was still furious but, to his credit, he wasn't yelling at her. He wasn't berating her. He wasn't even acknowledging she existed.

"How much longer do you think it will be?" She finally broke the silence.

"Not sure." Clay didn't even bother to turn around.

Jenny got up and walked over to stand by the window with him. She looked down on the parking lot. It was just starting to get light outside, just a hint of dawn colored the sky. She was exhausted. The night seemed to just go on and on, and all she wanted was for Nathan to wake up and be okay. Nothing else mattered.

Clay edged away from her.

"Clay, I'm sorry. I know that isn't enough, but I am sorry."

He ignored her. She put her hand on his arm, but he pulled away. "I don't know what else to say. You broke up with me and I was so scared. So alone. I was afraid of what my father might do. I was afraid he'd make me give up the baby. You know how my father is. Then Joseph said he'd marry me for a bit and then we'd divorce. It seemed like a way out at the time."

"You could have come to me."

"You said you wanted your freedom. I was supposed

to come back with 'no such luck, you're having a baby?'"

"I didn't know you were pregnant when I said that."

"You made it pretty clear you wanted nothing to do with me, that I'd been a high school fling. That you wanted your freedom and going out with me would hold you back. It would *interfere with your life*, I believe were your exact words." The words still stung. She could still remember the hurt. It had choked her, taken over her whole body until there had been nothing left but a dull, throbbing emptiness.

"You should've told me."

"Back then I thought I was doing the best thing for my child. I didn't want him to have a father who didn't want him. I didn't want Nathan to grow up feeling unwanted, or that he was interfering in someone's life. You need to understand. I was seventeen, unwed, and pregnant. My boyfriend had just told me he didn't want me. That I didn't fit into his future. There was no way I wanted to bring a baby into the middle of that." Jenny could feel the tears start to roll down her cheeks. She felt like she'd been crying all night. She wasn't even sure where they were coming from anymore, since she felt all dried up inside.

She turned when she heard a sound at the door. Two men entered, rolling Nathan in.

"Mom?"

His voice. Her son's wonderful voice. The blood raced through her, warming her, giving her hope. "Nathan, I'm right here." She rushed to his side and touched his cheek.

As they rolled his gurney into the room, she reluctantly stepped aside. The two men efficiently moved Nathan from the gurney to the bed and hung his IV at his bedside. Nathan watched them, looking confused.

"Mom, what happened?"

"You were in an accident."

"I was?" She saw confusion cloud his eyes. "I don't remember. Where were we? Are you okay?"

"I wasn't there. Just you and Danielle."

"I can't remember. Is Danielle okay?" He stopped for a few moments like he was struggling to get his thoughts together. "Where were we? Did we total Dad's car?"

"Shh. You need to rest. Danielle's okay. You just get some sleep. We'll talk when you feel better."

Nathan glanced over at Clay. "Why is he here?" But he drifted off to sleep before she could even think of how to answer his question.

Chapter Fourteen

Why *was* he here? Clay thought that was a question he'd love to answer, but he knew it wasn't the time or place.

He had waited until Jenny fell asleep in a chair in the corner of the room, before he crossed the room and stood beside Nathan's bed, staring down at him. This son of his.

He looked pale and fragile in the hospital bed. Swallowed up by generic white blankets and resting his head on a sterile, uncomfortable looking pillow. His hands were out of the covers though, and Clay looked at them in fascination. Strong looking hands with long, lean fingers. Clay finally allowed himself to look at his son's face, to take the time to actually stare at it and imprint it into his mind.

Nathan's face held a look of peaceful contentment, unaware, deep in sleep, of all he had gone through this past night. He moved slightly in his sleep, and Clay caught a glimpse of a scar on Nathan's chin. He wondered how his son had gotten it.

His son had brown hair, the same color as his mother. Thick hair, though he wore it cut short in an all-American-boy type haircut. No piercings, thank goodness. He couldn't reconcile himself to male piercings. He was just getting more conservative and set in his ways, he guessed. Though he realized, in the scheme of things, a pierced ear would have been the least of his worries.

He wished his son would open his eyes. He so wanted to look into his eyes. Wanted to see his smile. Hear his laugh. Talk to him and explain he hadn't known about him, that's why he hadn't been there for him. His heart caught in his chest. He hadn't been there to watch his first steps, teach him to play ball, read him books, watch him grow up. Joey had.

Another surge of anger washed over him. At Jenny, for keeping his son a secret, at her father for threatening him all those years ago, but mostly at the feeling of loss over all the months and years he'd missed with his son. He was mad at Joey, too, for never telling him. They had been best friends once. He'd never be able to forgive Jenny for doing this to him. He'd been hurt when she married Joey, and angry at both of them. It had hurt so badly he'd barely been able to function for weeks on end, but it was nothing like the anger he felt now. Anger at Jenny and Joey, rage at the fates. This was not something he believed he could ever work through or get over.

He looked over at Jenny, curled up in the chair, hugging herself tightly. He automatically got the extra blanket from the end of Nathan's bed before he could even stop himself, and crossed over and tucked it gently around her. She murmured in her sleep, but didn't wake up.

He had such a riotous flood of emotions in regard to this woman. He was mad at her, but at the same time felt the need to protect her. He felt empathy with her worry about her son. Their son. There were too many thoughts to sort out.

A tiredness he couldn't avoid seized him. He sank down into the empty chair across the room, thinking he'd just get a few quick moments of shut eye.

* * * * *

Jenny slowly woke up, struggling to bring her thoughts into focus, unsure where she was, but very aware her neck and back were screaming at her. She opened her eyes and sat straight up. Nathan. She must have fallen asleep in Nathan's room. The light was streaming in the window now, shining on her son sleeping peacefully in the bed. Thank goodness. Someone had covered her with a blanket. Clay? Somehow she doubted that.

She turned her head and saw Clay asleep in the chair across the room. He was frowning in his sleep and he looked like he could slide out of the chair at any moment. His face was lined with worry, even in sleep. A day's worth of beard covered his face, darkening it slightly. His clothes were a wrinkled mess, the front of his shirt stained with blood. From Danielle, she'd guess.

Glancing down, she realized she fared no better. She looked like she'd slept in her clothes, but then she had, hadn't she? She quietly slipped on her shoes and crossed over to where Nathan was sleeping. She stood there staring at him. She could look at him all day long. Drinking him in. Giving him her strength. She was just so glad he was alive. The doctor who had come in after Nathan was brought to the room was hopeful there wasn't any permanent damage from the head injury. Some short term memory loss of the accident, but that seemed to be all. They'd run more tests, of course, but things were looking good.

What she really needed was to wrap her arms around him and hold him forever. There was a bandage on his forehead, where the doctor had stitched a gash. She wondered if he'd have a scar. But with her next thought, she realized she didn't care. He was alive. That was all that mattered.

She turned when she heard Clay stirring. He opened his eyes and looked directly at her, then at Nathan. He stretched his arms over his head and sat up, leaning to one side then the other. He scrubbed his hands over his face and rolled his head forward and back. Then, with an athletic grace she had always marveled at, he pushed up out of the chair.

He crossed over and stood on the opposite side of Nathan's bed and stared down at their son. She watched a kaleidoscope of emotions cross his face, then observed his carefully placed look of detachment when he turned to her. His eyes no longer held the flashing blue anger. They were a cold steely blue now, deliberately devoid of emotion with an icy remoteness in their depths.

She turned away from those chilly eyes when she heard a low moan from her son.

Nathan stirred, then slowly opened his eyes. "Mom?" His voice quavered.

"I'm right here, sweetheart." She touched his face. "You doing okay?"

"I hurt." He coughed. "Everywhere."

"You're going to be sore for a while," Clay answered.

Nathan turned to look at Clay on the other side of his bed. "How come he's here?"

"He's a doctor. I asked him to come by. Besides, he's concerned about you."

Nathan reached his hand up to his head and touched the bandage. He seemed confused by the IV going into the back of his hand.

"They're giving you fluids and some pain meds," Clay said. "If you get uncomfortable, make sure you let your mom know. They'll give you something more for the pain."

"I thought you didn't like me."

Clay paused and Jenny watched him struggle to find

the right words. "I was hard on you. I'm sorry. I was worried about Danielle."

"But I got into an accident with her. Why aren't you madder at me now? Did I hit a tree or run off the road, or what? Did someone hit us? I don't remember what happened."

"It's okay to have some memory loss. You hit your head," Clay answered in his no-nonsense doctor voice.

"I remember going over and picking up Danielle. That's the last thing I remember. You're not mad about that?"

"Well, I asked you not to see her, but I realize Danielle is strong willed, to say the least. She said it was her idea."

"So you're mad at Danielle?"

"I'm just glad both of you are all right." Clay glanced at his watch. "You tell your mother if you need anything. I need to go stop by the house and check on Danielle and I have to go to the clinic. I'll reschedule what I can, then I'll be back."

"We'll see you later." Jenny watched him cross the room and stand in the doorway for a moment, looking at Nathan. Then he was gone. The room suddenly felt empty without Clay's presence. She realized that even though Clay was mad at her, she had appreciated having someone there beside her last night. Someone as worried about her son as she was, someone willing to sit by his side all night until he woke up.

* * * * *

"How's Nathan this morning?" Greta sat at the kitchen table drinking coffee and doing another one of her endless crossword puzzles.

"He's better. I still need to track down his doctor and talk to him." Clay poured himself a steaming cup of coffee from the old percolator.

"You look exhausted. Did you get any sleep?"

"Some. How's Danielle this morning?"

"I just peeked in on her. She's still asleep. She's really worried about what you're going to do. On the way home last night she couldn't quit crying."

"Stress reaction."

"Clay, she needs to know you still love her and understand she made a mistake."

"She knows I love her." He sat down beside his mom. "She knows that."

Greta sighed. "I think she needs to hear it. She needs to know that while you don't approve of what she did, you're still there for her."

He rubbed his hands along his day old growth of beard. "I'll talk to her later today. When she wakes up, tell her I'm not mad. Disappointed, but not mad."

"I'll tell her you're not mad, but you can do the disappointed routine on your own."

Clay took a long sip of coffee. "Mom, I need to tell you something about Nathan."

"Is he okay?" Greta sounded worried.

"Yes. I mean he's hurt, but he'll recover. It's not that.

It's something else."

"I already know." His mother reached over and covered his hand. "He's your son."

Clay pushed back his chair and stared at his mom. "You do? When did you find out? Why didn't you tell me?" *Did everyone know but him?*

"Jenny told me last night, but I had begun to suspect it already. There are times when he looks just like you. He has your eyes."

"He does?" Clay tried to picture Nathan's eyes. He couldn't even remember what color they were.

"They're blue."

"How did you…"

"I can read your face like a book, son." Greta smiled at him. "So, what are you going to do now?"

"I don't know. Jenny wants to wait until Nathan feels stronger to tell him. I understand that, but I want him to know. I want him to know *right now*."

"Jenny is right about waiting a bit until he is stronger."

"I know that. It's best for Nathan. But as soon as he's feeling better she has to tell him. Or I will."

"I think he needs to hear it from his mom."

Clay sighed. "I know. I'm just so angry right now. About all that has been taken away from me." He looked at his mother. "From you. Aren't you angry, too?"

Greta set down the crossword puzzle on the worn Formica table top. "I'm sorry I missed out on so much of Nathan's life. Yes, I'm sorry for that. But I do understand you'd just broken up with her and she was scared. Her father is a force to be reckoned with."

"Her father is a cold, heartless, human being. And that is being generous."

"Son, you can't blame this all on him."

"You don't know the whole story."

"Well, I'm here whenever you want to tell me."

His mom was like that, always there for him, never pushing him before he was ready. "We'll talk later. I'm just worn out now and I need to go get cleaned up and get to the clinic."

"I called Velda this morning and told her what happened. She's going to reschedule what she could and bump back your early morning appointments."

"Thanks, Mom. Call me if Danielle is having any problems when she wakes up. You could give her one of the pain pills the doctor prescribed if she needs it. Try to get her to eat a little something first."

* * * * *

"Hey, Doc. How's Danielle this morning?" Velda called out to him as he entered the clinic.

"She's still sound asleep."

"Well, that's probably best. She'll be a sore girl when she wakes up." Velda got up and pressed a steaming cup of coffee into his hands. "I bet you can use this. I moved your patients back. The first one will be here in about fifteen minutes. I rebooked all I could because I knew you'd be wanting to get out of here early today."

"Thanks, Velda. I don't know what I'd do without you."

"You wouldn't survive, trust me." Velda flashed him a warm smile. "How's Mrs. Bouchard's son doing?"

Clay caught his breath. Mrs. Bouchard's son. It hit him in the gut. His son. Not just Jenny's son. He wanted the world to know. He wanted to get to know this son, who he hadn't had a chance to get to know. He sighed. "He's holding his own. He woke up this morning. Some memory loss from last night, but that's common with a head injury. He looked good though. Tired, but alert."

"You went by to see him?"

"I stayed the night."

Before Velda could ask why he hadn't been at home taking care of his own daughter, Doc Baker pushed through the doorway. "Velda, my girl. How are things going?" His booming voice echoed in the waiting room.

"Just fine, Dr. B. How goes the vacation?"

"Well, the missus is driving me nuts with her mile long list of fix-it projects for the house. She acts like I never have time to fix anything."

Velda just raised her eyebrow and smiled.

"Clay, I heard about your daughter and Nathan Bouchard."

Not much was secret in the town of Comfort Crossing. This was being hammered home to Clay this week. Well, there was one secret. He had a son.

Dr. Baker reached out grasped Clay's hand in his firm

grip. "I thought you might like some help today."

"I don't want you giving up your vacation."

"Let's just say this would be a welcome vacation *from* my vacation." Dr. Baker grinned. "I can help out for the next few days, then the missus and I are headed out to visit the grandkids in Texas. Can't figure out where I went wrong that my kids would move to Texas. Next thing you know, they'll have on those cowboy hats and wear boots and… well, they'll become Texans." He grinned.

"I feel terrible you're giving up your vacation time but I do appreciate this. I could sure use your help for a few days."

"Thought you might. I enjoy this vacation stuff, but coming in for a few days is just what I need right now. Too bad this clinic can't be a part time job."

"This clinic is more than a full time job these days," Velda said. She picked up some charts. "Okay, here's the list of patients coming in. I'll feed them back to whichever one of you has an empty room. Okay?"

"Thank you. I really appreciate this." Clay shook Dr. Baker's hand.

"No problem, son. None at all. And don't quote me on this, but I think the missus will enjoy a little break from having me underfoot all day every day, too. Not that she'd ever admit it, since she's always nagging me to take time off."

The first patient pushed through the door with two blonde-headed boys in tow. "Doc Baker. You helping out Dr. Miller while his daughter recovers?"

"Dr. Miller, I was glad to hear your daughter is going to be okay."

No, there are few secrets in Comfort Crossing, Mississippi.

* * * * *

Danielle pushed through the doorway to Nathan's hospital room, followed by Greta and Abigail. Danielle was dressed in a much more conservative outfit than Jenny had seen her wear before. No long legs sticking out from an impossibly short skirt, no belly skin showing. She was obviously trying to avoid any confrontation with her father. Jenny pressed a finger to her lips so they wouldn't wake up Nathan. The nurse had given him some pain meds a while ago, and he had drifted off into a peaceful sleep.

Danielle walked over to the side of the bed and looked down at Nathan. A lone tear trailed down her cheek. She mouthed the words "I'm sorry." She wiped the tear away.

Jenny nodded toward the door and the four of them crossed out to the hallway. Abigail tugged on Jenny's sleeve and then gave her a hug and a smile.

"Thanks, Abigail." Jenny smiled back at the child. Abigail's face was lined with little girl worry. Her shoulders looked like she carried the world on them. Such a serious little girl. She'd had to deal with more than her share of heartbreak in her young life. "Don't worry, sweetheart. He'll be okay. He just needs to sleep for a while and get stronger."

"How is he?" Danielle's voice sounded dangerously near the breaking point.

Jenny gave her a hug. "He's going to be fine. He doesn't remember the accident though. Your father said that's common with a head injury."

Danielle stood there, her face holding a look Jenny couldn't quite peg. "He doesn't remember? Anything?"

"No, but your dad said not to worry about that. Okay? He's going to be okay. You'll have to help him learn how to use his crutches. He broke his ankle."

"I'll do anything. I'm so sorry. I'm so stupid. You must hate me."

"I don't hate you."

Danielle collapsed into her arms, crying softly now. "I'm so sorry. I shouldn't have called him to come get me… and it's all my fault."

"It's not all your fault, Danielle. He was drinking and driving. You're lucky he didn't kill both of you, or someone else."

Danielle went quiet and the tears slipped down her face again. "It's my fault. Are you really mad at Nathan?"

"I'm disappointed in him. I might ground him until he's thirty or so. He'll not be doing any more driving for a good long time. He'll lose his license and I don't know what else will happen. But I'm just so glad you both are going to be okay. That's all I want. He made a really poor choice. Kids do that. He'll have to pay the consequences.

But I love him."

"I'm so sorry. You'll tell Nathan that when he wakes up, won't you?"

"Of course I will." She held the girl in her arms while she calmed down. "You'll be able to tell him yourself when he's better."

"He probably hates me."

"No, I'm sure he doesn't. He has already been asking about you."

"He has?" Danielle pulled away and dashed the tears from her face.

"He wanted to know if you were okay."

"Did you tell him I was fine?"

Jenny nodded. "As soon as he comes home, you can tell him yourself." If Clay would let Danielle see Nathan. Jenny was somehow sure Greta had brought the girls here to see Nathan today without asking Clay, unwilling to have him say no. Greta seemed to know Danielle needed to see Nathan was okay.

What was Clay going to do now? He was so furious at Nathan for drinking and driving, but now he knew that anger was aimed at his own son. And when the secret was out, he couldn't keep Nathan away from Danielle for the rest of their lives. They had to figure out some way for everyone to deal with the truth.

Unless Clay decided to reject Nathan, like he'd rejected her so many years ago. But she'd seen that look in his eyes when he stood by Nathan's bedside this morning. A father worried about his son.

"Come on, girls, I better get Danielle back home. I think this was enough excitement for one day."

Jenny looked at the girl. Her face was drawn and pinched. "Are you in pain?"

"No, I'm okay." Danielle didn't sound convincing.

"Are you sure?"

"I'm sure." The girl's face held a haunted look.

"It will be okay."

"I'm so sorry." Danielle leaned against her grandmother. "Let's go, Grams."

* * * * *

Bella slipped into Nathan's hospital room. Jenny was asleep in the chair near the window. She crossed over to the hospital bed and stared down at the sleeping boy. He looked so innocent, lying there in the bed. But Jenny was going to have to help him deal with the fall out of drinking and driving.

Poor Jenns. She just couldn't catch a break. But thank goodness Nathan was going to be all right.

She turned when she heard Jenny stir. Jenny looked up and smiled at her. A weak smile, but a smile nonetheless. Bella crossed the room and sank into the chair beside her friend.

"I came as soon as I heard."

"Thanks."

"Becky Lee said that Nathan is going to be okay, but has some memory loss of the accident. A broken ankle, too."

"Yes, he'll be okay. He'll be sore for a while. But thank goodness he'll be okay."

Bella took in her friend's exhausted look and wrinkled clothes. Her tired, tired eyes. "You look terrible."

"Gee, thanks."

"No, seriously, you should go home and get some rest."

"I can't leave Nathan."

"You can't get so worn down you can't take care of him when he comes home."

Jenny shrugged. "I told him."

"Told who, what?"

Jenny lowered her voice. "I told Clay that Nathan was his son. He was furious, of course. I told him I'd tell Nathan as soon as he gets stronger."

Bella reached over and squeezed Jenny's hand, wishing she could give her friend strength. "Well, I'm glad the secret is out. It was time."

"I don't know what is going to happen now." Jenny ran her hand through her hair.

"We'll take it one step at a time. Becky Lee and I will be with you. Every step. It's going to be okay."

"I don't know what's going to happen to Nathan, legally. With the accident. With Clay being his father. It's all so messed up. And I don't understand Nathan drinking and driving. I thought he had settled down. Dealt with everything. Now, I'm going to throw more turmoil in his life." Jenny's eyes held a haunted look.

"Has Sheriff Dawson been by?"

"Not since last night."

"Well, let's just concentrate on getting Nathan better. Then we'll work on the rest."

Jenny nodded.

It broke Bella's heart to see her friend in so much pain. She wished she could fix things for her. She'd kept Jenny's secret for all these years, never once questioning her decision, and she'd be there for her now, too. Now that the secret was out.

Chapter Fifteen

Nathan came home a few days later, and except for the crutches and the fact he had stitches in his forehead, you'd never know he'd been in an accident. He said he was still sore all over, but otherwise he was doing fine.

Clay had been at the hospital every morning and evening. Nathan seemed confused by why Clay was there, but had stopped asking about it. Clay brought him magazines to keep him busy. They watched a baseball game one evening, though both agreed the Mets deserved to lose it. They weren't on their game, that night, whatever on their game meant. Jenny had just sat in the corner, pretending to read the paper, but secretly watching the two of them together.

Greta had insisted on bringing over dinner tonight. She said Jenny had enough to do with bringing Nathan home and getting him all settled in.

Jenny had surprised herself by saying why don't they

all come over, then, Greta, Clay and the girls. Nathan would enjoy the company. She wondered if she asked them all just to placate Clay, to give him a reason to come over and see Nathan, but keep him from pressuring her to tell Nathan the truth. She needed to give Nathan time to get stronger. Or maybe she needed to give *herself* time to get stronger. She freely admitted to herself that the last few days had taken their toll, worrying about Nathan, telling Clay and dealing with his anger. She'd aged years in the last few days.

"Mom?" Nathan called from the couch, where she'd made him a nice comfy place to lie and watch TV. Though he had taken a two hour nap that afternoon. The trip home from the hospital had tired him out.

He was in no condition to hear the truth yet.

She walked into the family room with a glass of milk and some cookies. "Good afternoon, sleepyhead."

"I can't believe I slept so long."

"You needed it." She looked at his leg, propped up on the pillow, and the crutches leaning against the wall. He'd been so lucky. "Here, are you hungry?" She placed the plate of cookies and the glass of milk on the coffee table beside the couch, in easy reach for him.

"Drink some milk." She had this absurd need for him to drink milk, sure that the calcium would heal his broken bones faster.

Nathan took a small sip of the milk. "What time are Danielle and her family coming over?"

"About five or so. That was very nice of Greta to offer to bring dinner."

"Danielle's grandmother is cool."

"I'd have to agree with you on that one." Jenny fluffed the pillows behind Nathan so he could sit up and have his snack.

"Is Danielle's father coming for sure?"

"Unless he gets tied up at the clinic."

"You think now I'm home from the hospital he's going to yell at me for the accident?"

Jenny wasn't sure of that herself. She knew Clay was mad about Nathan's drinking and driving, she was mad about it herself. Scared he had made that decision to drink and drive. But the overwhelming relief that both kids had survived overshadowed her anger. She'd deal with the consequences of his actions soon. No driving at all, and working to pay for the repairs to the car, if it could even be fixed. The estimates on the damage weren't in yet. Deal with whatever legal mess came out of the accident.

She realized Nathan was still waiting for an answer. "No, he won't yell at you." She wasn't sure it sounded convincing, even to her ears.

Nathan sighed and reached for a cookie. "I bet he does." He leaned back on the couch and picked up the remote. She saw him glance at the clock in anticipation or with apprehension. She wasn't sure which one.

Greta and the girls showed up about five o'clock

loaded down with ham, home baked bread, a veggie casserole and a big chocolate cake.

"Wow, great." Jenny held open the door.

"Just let me pop the ham and the casserole in your oven to keep it warm. Clay said he'd get here as soon as he could."

"That's fine." Jenny turned to the girls. "Nathan is in the family room. Go on in."

Danielle set down the cake. "Come on, Abby, let's see how he's doing." Abigail set down a paper sack beside the cake.

"I brought salad fixings, too."

"You brought a feast, Greta."

"I figured Nathan would like some home cooking after all that hospital food."

"I'm sure he will. It was nice of you to bring all this."

Greta looked towards the doorway to the family room. The sound of Danielle talking and Nathan laughing drifted into the kitchen. "I kind of liked cooking for my grandson."

"Greta, I'm so sorry about all of this. All this time…"

"Not another word. I didn't say that to make you feel guilty. We'll have plenty enough time to get to know each other. I made my share of poor choices when I was a teen."

"Thank you." Jenny didn't know what else to say. Greta was taking the news a lot better than Clay was, that's for sure.

Greta peeked her head through the doorway to check on the kids, and bustled back into the kitchen. "I'll get the salad made up, then maybe we can sit out on the porch for a bit before dinner."

"What can I do to help?"

"You get me a big bowl, a knife and your cutting board, and then you just sit down. You look exhausted."

Jenny found what Greta needed, then sank down gratefully on the bright cushion tied to the oak kitchen chair. She was tired. It had been a stressful few days. Now she was worried about Clay coming over tonight. She knew he wanted her to tell Nathan the truth, but she had told him she needed a few more days.

"I love your kitchen. Very homey." Greta stood at the kitchen sink washing the lettuce.

"I do love the house, though I considered selling it. It has so many memories. And it's really too big for just Nathan and I. It's hard for me to keep up with all the repairs and maintenance, even with Nathan helping with the yard work. I just don't know where I would move. My parents suggested we move in with them." Jenny laughed. "That's just not going to happen, even though I'm sure mother would enjoy the company, and could probably use some help with Father. I just can't do that to Nathan though. Move him into such a critical household."

"Um, hm." Greta just kept on making the salad and letting Jenny talk.

"Joseph's parents wanted us to move in with them, too. They have that big old house and they'd love to have Nathan there. But I couldn't hurt my parents like that. Taking Joseph's parents up on their offer, but turning down my own parents. It just seemed easier to stay here."

"I hear your father isn't doing so well."

"He's very sick. I'm not sure how much longer he'll make it. It's so strange to see him so frail and in need of help to do the simplest things. He was just always so... dynamic and in control of everything."

"I bet it's hard to see him that way."

"I do love him. But when I became an adult and had Nathan, I realized I didn't like my father very much as a person. He's very demanding and critical."

"Um..."

"He bosses my mother around like she doesn't matter much to him. I just don't want Nathan brought up in a house like that." Jenny traced the grain in the oak table top. "I guess you think I'm terrible for talking about my father like that."

"I think you're just being honest with yourself and doing what you think is best for your child. That's all a mother can do." Greta's voice held no recrimination in it. The sound of rhythmic chopping was the only sound in the kitchen, along with some filtered laughter from the family room.

"There, let me pop this in the fridge."

"I made some sweet tea. Would you like some?" Jenny

stood up.

"I reckon that would just hit the spot."

Jenny snagged some tall glasses from the cabinet, ice from the freezer, and poured them two large glasses of ice cold tea. She crossed over to the family room and let the kids know there was pop and tea in the fridge if they wanted any. She went out to join Greta on the porch. Choo Choo followed along behind them and settled down by the front porch steps.

They sat and talked about the kids, and school, and teaching. Jenny had forgotten how easy Greta was to talk to. She had missed the long hours she'd spent at Greta's home as a teen. Greta's home had always been warm and inviting. They had spent most of their time in the kitchen or out on Greta's porch. Jenny smiled at the memories.

"I've missed you, Jenny." Greta rocked slowly in the white wicker rocker.

"I've missed you, too."

* * * * *

Clay pulled into the long, tree lined driveway to Jenny's house. Jenny and Joey's house, he corrected. The man who had been dad to the son Clay had never known existed until this week. As he rounded the turn, he saw his mother and Jenny sitting on the front porch, looking for all the world like a mother-in-law and daughter-in-law, passing the time before dinner was ready. The thought stabbed at him, taunting him with what ifs.

Greta looked up and waved at him as he pulled up in

front of the house. Jenny didn't.

Clay sighed. It had been a long day at the clinic and, as much as he wanted to spend time with Nathan, it was exhausting to be around Jenny. There was so much tension between them.

He also worried about Nathan, and what Nathan thought of him. He was sure Danielle had told stories of how unfair he was, how hard he was on her. But then he had also been worried about Danielle the last few days. She'd been the perfect angel, helping Greta with chores, no loud stereo blaring from her room. She had even taken to wearing clothes he approved of. Heck, he didn't even know she owned some of the outfits she had been wearing. He hadn't seen her belly or her bra strap in days. Frankly, the new Danielle scared him to death. He didn't know what was up with her.

He crossed the distance to the porch in a few long strides and climbed the brick stairs. The porch stretched the length of the house and wrapped around the sides, deep and inviting. The large southern magnolia tree at the corner of the house shielded the porch from the late afternoon sun.

"Here, you sit down, son." Greta got up and motioned to a chair between her and Jenny. "Jenny, you just stay right there. I'll go in and get Clay a tall glass of sweet tea."

"I can get it," Jenny protested.

"No, you just sit there and let me do this. You look so tired."

"Thanks, Greta."

"Thanks, Mom." Clay looked at Jenny as he sank down into an incredibly comfortable chair with overstuffed cushions. Jenny did look tired. She had tiny worry lines creasing the corners of her eyes. She signed heavily, probably worried what he'd say to her. What was he going to say to her? It seemed like it all had been said.

"How's Nathan doing today?" He sank deeper into the chair. It felt good to be off his feet.

"He's doing okay. He's so glad to be home."

"I bet."

"The girls are in there keeping him entertained."

"That's nice." Could the conversation get any more bland?

"It looks like it's going to storm." Jenny nodded to the clouds gathering to the west.

Okay, yes, it could get even more insipid. They were reduced to discussing the weather. He was saved from further inane chitchat by Abigail, who pushed through the screen door, letting it slam behind her, and threw herself into his lap.

"Hey, pumpkin." Her hair smelled of flowers and her cheeks glowed a rosy pink. She hugged him. He wrapped his arms around her and hugged right back. "I missed you too, sweetie."

He turned when he heard the screen door squeak open again and the syncopated rhythm of Nathan walking through the doorway on crutches. Danielle carefully held the door open for him, and caught the screen door before it had a chance to slam shut.

Jenny rose from her seat. "Nathan, are you sure you're up for this?"

"Mom, I can't spend the rest of my life on the couch. Besides, Danielle helped me. I'm fine."

"Well, take my chair," Jenny insisted.

Clay got up and crossed over to pick up a footrest. "Here. Put your foot up on this. It helps to keep it elevated." He placed it in front of the chair Nathan had taken. Jenny and Nathan's dog got up and crossed over and sat down beside Nathan. Clay didn't even know the name of his son's dog.

"What's your dog's name?"

"Choo Choo." Danielle answered for Nathan. See, his daughter knew more about his son than he did.

Greta came out and pressed a glass of tea into his hands, then sat down again. Clay turned around and found Danielle had sat down in his chair. Nathan was in Jenny's and Abigail perched on the edge of the footrest.

That left only the porch swing for him and Jenny. He watched Jenny process the same bit of information just a fraction of a moment after he did. She glanced at the swing, looking like she was ready to bolt to safety.

"Jenny, hon, sit down. You too, Clay. You both look dead on your feet." Greta motioned to the swing.

Jenny slowly crossed the white planking of the porch and slipped into the swing. Clay knew of no way to avoid it, so he crossed over and sank down beside her. There wasn't enough room for him to keep his distance. His leg brushed up against her thigh. A flash of electricity raced through the skin on his leg and he ached to reach over and just touch her leg.

No, he didn't. He was mad at her.

The fresh smell of lavender attacked his senses, mocking him. Jenny had always loved lavender. Soap. Lotion. Perfume. The lavender aroma beat his senses now, laughing at his meager attempts to ignore it.

He looked over at his son. Focus. On anything but lavender. "You feeling okay today, Nathan?"

"Pretty good, sir. Glad to be home. But I'm starving. The hospital food suc— wasn't very good."

"Dinner will be ready in about twenty minutes." Greta sipped her tea, the ice cubes rattling around the glass, filling the pause in the conversation.

Sir. His son called him sir. He was probably afraid Clay would let loose on him for drinking and driving. He would have a conversation with him about it, later, after Nathan knew the truth and they'd found some kind of footing between them. He was still mad at the boy. He could have killed his daughter. Heck, he could have killed his *son*.

Clay looked around. Danielle was uncharacteristically quiet. Jenny held herself in stone-like silence, her arms wrapped across her body. He rubbed his face. The tension between everyone crackled like the lightening in the distance.

Nathan was the first to break the silence. "I'm sorry, sir."

Everyone on the porch turned and looked at him. Clay could feel Jenny tense up even more besides him.

Greta, he could tell, took in the situation in one quick glance and stood up. "Abigail, honey, why don't you come help Grams finish up dinner?" Abigail got up and reached for her grandmother's hand and they disappeared into the house.

Nathan continued as soon as the screen door closed. "I shouldn't have been drinking and driving. It was stupid. And I know not being able to remember what happened, or why I was drinking, is no excuse."

Clay felt Jenny's hand press on his leg. He turned to look at her and her face held a warning. He turned back to Nathan. "I am disappointed. You two could have been hurt a lot worse, or killed."

"I don't know why I did it. I got kind of out of control when my dad died, but it hurt Mom a bunch when I got into trouble. I'm not sure why I decided to drink that night. I'm sorry."

Clay bristled at Nathan calling Joey his dad. He was actually at a loss at what to say. Before he could come up with the right way to handle it all, Danielle broke in.

"Don't yell at him, Dad."

"I wasn't going to."

"It was my fault."

"I know you called him and snuck out. That was wrong too, but—"

Danielle's face crumpled into tears. They streamed down her face. "No, you have it—" She gulped a breath of air. "You have it all wrong." She turned towards Nathan. "I'm so sorry, Nathan. I should have told them before. I was afraid."

"Afraid of what?" Clay asked her.

"Afraid of you." The tears welled in her eyes, her sobs almost choking off her words.

Clay sat back in shock. "You aren't *afraid* of me."

"I was afraid you'd send me off to live with Mom... and Mom doesn't want me." Danielle was sobbing quietly now. "Nathan, you must hate me, too."

"It's okay, Danielle. I'm not mad you called me to come get you. I could have said no."

"No, would you all *listen* to me. It's my fault. *Mine.*" Danielle jumped up and pulled at the collar of her top. She wrenched it off her left shoulder. "See this?"

Clay looked at the angry bruise on her shoulder. "That's from the shoulder harness." Then he paused as the reality of what she was saying hit him. Her left shoulder. Left.

His daughter continued. "Nathan wasn't driving. *I* was driving. I was drinking. It was my bottle. I grabbed Nathan's keys. He was trying to stop me." She whirled to face Nathan. "I know you hate me now. I should have told the truth before this."

"I don't hate you, Danielle." Nathan's voice held a soothing tone. "I'm glad you told me now though. I couldn't believe I was doing this to my mom again. Causing this kind of trouble."

"Danielle. You were driving Nathan's car?" Clay stared at his daughter.

She broke into tears again. "Yes. It's all my fault."

"Were you driving because Nathan was drunk?"

"No, Daddy. Nathan wasn't drinking. I was. I took a bottle of some kind of liquor from Grams."

"You were?" Clay's head reeled, he didn't think he could stand another shock this week. His thoughts were jumbled, his nerves were shot. He glanced over at Jenny and saw she was doing no better than he was. Her tired, pale face had two bright spots of color on her cheeks. He heard her suck in a breath of air.

"I called Nathan to come get me, and snuck out the window. I was so mad at you for saying I couldn't see Nathan. He said he couldn't come, but then I told him I was going out on my own. So he said to wait and he would be there. I met him down on the road, and we went out by some stream. I drank the booze, but Nathan wouldn't. Then I stole his keys and got into the driver's seat. I said I wanted to drive the cool sports car." She paused and wiped away her tears. "Nathan jumped in the passenger side and told me to stop. But I laughed at him. I took off down the road. He reached over and tried to stop me. I went around a curve and lost control. He didn't have his seatbelt on because he was trying to reach over and get me to stop." Danielle turned to Jenny. "Mrs. Bouchard, you must hate me, too."

Jenny pushed off the swing and crossed over to the girl and pulled her into her arms. "No, I don't. I'm glad you told us now." She patted Danielle's back then set her gently away and pushed the blonde hair away from her face. She touched Danielle's chin and gently tilted her face up. "I'm not mad. I'm so glad you both are alive. I think you've learned your lesson. Nothing I could do or say would be worse than what you already went through. I'm sure there will be no more drinking and driving in your future."

"Never again. I swear." Danielle sobbed the words.

Clay knew he should be the one saying this to his daughter. Jenny was saying exactly the right things. Her warm brown eyes were filled with pain and hurt—for Danielle. For his daughter's pain. After he'd been so hard on Nathan. Guilt and remorse twisted through Clay.

Jenny smiled at Danielle. "We all make bad choices when we're young. It happens. It's part of growing up. We do the best we can and try to learn from our mistakes. We try to make amends for any harm that comes from our choices."

Clay knew Jenny was talking as much to him, as to Danielle. He pushed off the swing and crossed over to his daughter in two strides and pulled her into his arms. "It's going to be okay, Danielle. I'm not sending you away.

Ever. There is nothing you can ever do that would make me stop loving you." And he prayed his daughter would believe him, that he could find a way to convince her nothing she ever did would make him stop loving her.

His daughter cried softly against his shirt while he stroked her hair. How had they reached this point? Where his daughter was afraid of him and thought she'd be sent away. He was such a fool, of course she'd be worried about that after her mother had left them.

"I love you, Danielle." He gruffly murmured it against his beautiful daughter's blonde hair.

"I love you too, Daddy."

Chapter Sixteen

Two more days at home and Jenny could tell Nathan was going stir crazy. He'd even convinced her to let him drive over to visit Joseph's parents. Not by himself, of course. She had ridden with him. He insisted that since it was his left ankle that was broken, with a cast only to his knee, that he'd be fine to drive. She didn't want him to be afraid to get in a car, or to drive. But she had clutched the car seat the whole way over to the Bouchards' house, the whole five minutes, tops, it had taken to get there.

Life seemed fragile again these days, the way it had when they had found out about Joseph's cancer and realized it wasn't responding to any of the treatments. Every detail of the days was in sharper focus. The intense heat of the summer noontime sun. The chirping of the birds at the bird feeder. The dark green smoothness of the leaves on the gardenia bush outside her door, and the velvety whiteness of its flowers.

It was time, past time, really. And Clay was issuing vague ultimatums. She was going to tell Nathan today. No more excuses. No more hiding. She grabbed the two glasses of lemonade and walked out to the porch where Nathan was sitting and looking at some car magazine.

"Hey, sweetheart. I brought you some lemonade."

Her son looked up. His smile reached all the way to his beautiful blue eyes. His brown hair was tousled from the breeze that thankfully blew today, chasing away the oppressive heat of the last few days. "Thanks, Mom."

"I need to talk to you." Jenny sat down in the chair across from her son and reached over to hand him the lemonade. Her heart did its traitorous zydeco rhythm as she gathered her courage.

"What about?" Nathan put down his magazine.

"It's about you." She took a deep breath and pressed her hands on the armrests of the chair.

"What did I do?" He looked confused.

"Nothing. It's not like that." She paused, searching for the words she had been trying to find for days. She had played this scene over and over in her head the last year, but it never ended right. It was always a disaster. She just prayed that this time, the real time, it would work out.

"Then what's up?" Nathan took a swig of the cool drink.

"It's about you. And Joseph."

"Dad and me?"

"Nathan, I don't know how to tell you this." The

moment of truth was here and she was more scared than she'd ever been in her life. It was harder than telling Clay. Her hands shook and she pressed them against her legs. She was about to rock the very foundation her son had built his life on. She couldn't bear to cause him this pain. Her heart pounded and tears chased at the corners of her eyes. But she would not cry. She'd tell him the truth.

"Mom, would you just spit it out?"

Her heart hammered in her chest, she could barely breath. He was right. Just spit it out. Carefully. "Nathan, I was already pregnant when I married Joseph."

"Mom, this is not going to be one of those sex talks, is it? About being careful? You already gave me the lecture." Nathan laughed then. "You think I'm going to be shocked because you and Dad had sex before you were married?"

"No, it's not that." Jenny set down her glass. "I was pregnant with another man's child. Not Joseph's."

"So what happened to that kid, did you lose him? Miscarry, I mean. Or give him up for adoption?"

She had so messed this up. "Nathan, I was pregnant with *you*. Joseph is not your biological father."

Nathan took a sip of lemonade and spilled it down the front of his shirt. "You're lying." He slammed the glass down on the coffee table. "What are you talking about? Of course he's my dad."

"Well, he's your dad, but not your biological one."

"You lied all this time?" Her son's voice held a tone of

sharp anger. "Why are you telling me this now?" Then he looked at her, his eyes flashing with hurt and anger. "Did Dad know this?"

"Yes, Joseph knew before he asked me to marry him."

"I don't get it. He asked you to marry him knowing you were going to have some other guy's baby?"

"Yes, he did."

"But why?"

"So you'd have a name. To protect me from my father's anger. So people in town wouldn't gossip about you. For a whole lot of reasons. He loved you so, Nathan, from the first moment he took you in his arms. You were his whole world." She choked back tears, willing herself to go on.

"So who is my real father?"

A wave of trepidation, no, outright fear, rolled over her. Her next sentence would seal their future forever, nothing would ever be the same. She looked at her son, sitting there, his eyes flashing the same steel blue as his father. So like him. "Your father is—" Her voice broke and she tried again. "Your father is Clay Miller."

"Dr. Miller?" He pushed out of the chair and reached for his crutches. "He's my father? Danielle's dad?"

"Yes."

"Why didn't you tell me before this?" Her son's eyes flashed with unconcealed anger and hurt.

"I did what I thought was best at the time. I was so young, Nathan. Scared." Her heart hammered against her ribs and she grabbed the arms of the chair.

"So Dr. Miller didn't want me? Was that it?"

Jenny rushed to explain. Nothing was coming out right. "No, that's not it at all. He didn't know I was pregnant."

"Does he know it now?" He shook his head. "Of course he does, that's why he's been hanging around."

"I just told Clay he was your father. When you were in the hospital." She reached out to him. "Nathan, I tried to do what I thought was right for you."

"Lying to me was right? Save it." His tone was shorter than he'd ever used with her. She stood up and reached out to comfort him, but he jerked away from her touch. "Leave me alone." He turned his back on her and thumped into the house.

She stared out into the yard, her heart feeling like it was ripped from inside of her. Without really comprehending what she was doing, she walked inside and wandered around the house. Picking up the trophy Nathan won in baseball. Running her hand along the rim of the ashtray he had made out of tiles in kindergarten, even though neither she nor Joseph smoked. Adjusting the picture on the mantle of Joseph with Nathan, at about a year old, riding on his dad's shoulders. Joseph had been a great dad to Nathan. She hoped Nathan remembered that and realized how much Joseph had loved him.

She went upstairs to the bedroom she no longer

shared with Joseph. The room mocked her with loneliness. After Joseph had died, she had changed the bedspread to a yellow floral one. She'd bought ruffled pillow shams and matching curtains. She'd put a big potted fern in the corner, and a floral print recliner beside the window. Anything to make it look different and not so achingly empty.

She heard Nathan go downstairs, but she knew she should give him some space, some time to process all the news she had sprung on him today. She longed to take him in her arms and assure him everything would work out, that she hadn't meant to hurt him. That Joseph had loved him. She yearned for the days when a kiss on a booboo and cartoon character bandage could solve her son's hurt.

There were no tears left in her to cry. The pain was too deep for tears. She'd give anything to protect her son from the hurt he was going through now. She crossed over to the bathroom and flipped the smooth steel handle on the faucet, staring at the water rushing into the sink. The cool water rushed over her hands, and she bent down and splashed it on her face. She reached for a fluffy hand towel and dried off.

The sound of a car engine turning over pulled her from her thoughts. She rushed to the window and threw it open. "Nathan!"

It was too late. Her son squealed the tires as he backed the car out and headed down the drive. Her world cantilevered out of control while she watched the car disappear down the driveway.

* * * * *

Clay would give Jenny one more day. That was it. She could tell Nathan, or he would tell his son himself if Jenny couldn't bring herself to do it. But Nathan would be told. Twenty-four hours. That was it. And he'd told Jenny this.

"Daddy, what's wrong?" Danielle came up beside him as he stood at the sink drying the dinner dishes.

He looked at his daughter. She seemed so different this last week, quieter, but in some ways more assured of herself. Like she finally believed he wouldn't send her away, wouldn't desert her like her mother had. It didn't even take a psychology degree for him to realize that was the reason she had been acting out and getting into trouble all this time. She was testing him, to see if he'd still want her, or if he would leave her. He couldn't believe it had taken him so long to figure this out.

"Nothing's wrong."

"You look sad or something."

"No. I'm fine."

His daughter crossed over to the fridge and took out a pop. "You sure?"

"I'm sure."

He watched as she tapped the top of the can twice with her slender fingers, then popped the tab. She always did that, the two tap thing. He wondered where she had picked that up. He wondered why it was registering now.

He found himself marvelling at all the little things she did these days. The way she twirled her hair around her finger when she was nervous and crooked her mouth in a tiny half smile. The way she patted Abigail's hand when they sat and played Crazy Eights. How she brushed a kiss on her Gram's cheek before she went up to bed each night.

He felt like he had missed out on so much of the girls' growing up. He'd always been busy at work, working long, hard hours. When Claire left them, he'd been forced to shoulder a much bigger responsibility. He'd taken over all the day to day chores of parenthood. Slowly, over the past year, he'd come to know his daughters better than he ever had. He knew when Abigail was upset now, without her saying a word, especially since she wouldn't say anything at all now. He knew when Danielle was having a good day by the way she hummed under her breath.

He realized with a start, at that very moment, he could get to know Nathan like this, even missing out on all the years he had. He could learn to read his moods and take him to baseball games and do things with him. They could have a father son relationship. He would make it work. Somehow.

But first Nathan had to know the truth. He placed the last dish on the drain board and swore for the tenth time since they'd gotten here he was going to talk his mom into getting a dishwasher.

The phone rang and he crossed the kitchen to snatch it off the hook, hoping it wasn't an emergency. He'd really like to go in and join in the game of Crazy Eights that Greta and the girls were playing in the family room.

"Hello?" He tucked the phone under his chin.

"Clay, it's Jenny." He held his breath. Was she calling to tell him that she had spoken to Nathan?

"I told him." Clay's heart beat harder and he wiped his hand on the dish towel he clutched in his hands.

"What happened? I mean, how is he? How did he take the news?" He'd finally be able to talk to his son—as his son. He knew the truth.

"He's upset."

No surprise there. The boy had had curve ball after curve ball thrown at him this last year.

"He left, Clay."

"What do you mean he left?"

"I was upstairs, and he drove off in the car."

"You let him drive when he was upset?"

"I didn't *let* him drive off. He took the keys. I'd never knowingly let him drive when he's that upset."

Clay could hear the anger in her voice. She sounded like the littlest thing would push her over the edge. He wasn't going to be the one to do it. He carefully controlled his voice, without showing a hint of blame. "How long ago?"

"A couple of hours. I'm getting worried."

"Any idea where he might go?"

"I called Joseph's parents without really letting on what was going on. He's not there. I called around to some friends. No one has seen him. I was hoping he's with Danielle…"

"No, she's here playing cards in the next room." He paused. "No, she's really here, this time, Jenny. I just saw her."

"I don't know what to do. I'm so worried."

He could hear that in her voice. He was worried too. His son had just found out he was his father, and he'd run off when he heard the news. Not the start he had hoped for, that's for sure.

"Give me a couple of minutes. I'll come right over."

There was silence on the other end of the phone, then Jenny said, "Thank you, Clay."

The soft click of the phone being hung up filtered across the wires. He hung up his phone and crossed to the family room to tell his mom he was going out.

He grabbed his keys and wallet and rushed out to the car. As he drove down the highway and over the railroad tracks separating the wrong side of town from the rich side of town, he shook his head at how his life was unfolding. Why he had ever let Jenny's father convince him he wasn't good enough for Jenny? Why living on one side of the tracks made someone any more of a special person, than living on the other side. He'd been a stupid, clueless kid to let himself be intimidated by Old

Man Delacroix, and they were all paying the price now. He was mad at Jenny for not telling the truth, but he was possibly madder at himself for letting Jenny's father force him into breaking up with her.

He pulled in the drive to Jenny's house not fifteen minutes later. She was waiting for him on the front porch, dressed in a simple print sundress, looking very much like the girl he had once been so in love with.

"Have you heard from him?" Clay bounded up the stairs.

"Not a word."

"Cell phone?"

"He left it here."

In the fading light he could see the lines of worry etched on her face. She looked scared and alone. It hit him then, probably exactly how she had felt when she found out she was pregnant with Nathan and he had told her he didn't want her, that he wanted his freedom.

"Ah, Jenns." He took her into his arms. She melted against him. "We'll find him." He stroked her hair, giving her time to gain strength from him, trying to show her that he was there for her—this time.

"I'm so scared. It's just like the other night when he was missing."

"No, it's not. There isn't going to be an accident tonight. He probably just needed time to himself."

"He's so angry with me. He said I lied to him. I *did* lie to him. His whole life was built on a lie."

The heat of her body dissipated when she abruptly pulled back and looked into his eyes. "I've hurt him. I've hurt you. I don't know how to make it right."

"Well, first thing, the tears are going to stop." He had seen more tears from her in the last few days than he'd seen in all the years they had dated. He looked at her closely, sensing she was on the edge. "If you can."

The corner of her mouth tilted up just a touch.

"Then we're going to go out looking for him."

"But what if he comes back here?"

"You can leave him a note telling him to call your cell."

"I don't know if he'd even call."

"Well, we'll just keep driving back by the house, in between looking around for him."

She looked at him with such appreciation. Her eyes reflected how thankful she was to let him shoulder some of the responsibility. It must have been hard on her, this last year without Joseph, dealing with Nathan acting up. Doing it alone. He knew how hard it was, because he had done almost the same thing the last year.

"Okay, what's his curfew?"

"About eleven-thirty. But I don't think he's going to pay much attention to that tonight."

"Grab your cell phone and we'll go see if we can spot your car."

Jenny disappeared into the house, her skirt swishing briskly against her legs as she slid through the doorway.

Within moments she was back outside with her purse and her cell phone clutched in her hands. "I'm ready."

He took her elbow, more out of habit than anything else, and helped her down the stairs. As he opened the car door for her, she turned to him and looked him directly in the eyes. He lost himself for a brief moment in those honey brown eyes, but her voice pulled him back from their smoky depths. "Clay, thank you. I mean it. I just feel so... lost."

"We'll find him, Jenns. Or he'll come home after he's had some time to sort it all out. It was a lot to process. Joey not being his father, finding out I am. He probably feels like he's lost Joey all over again."

Jenny slipped into the car and looked up at him. "I know. I never imagined it would turn out like this. I've made such a mess of everyone's life."

He couldn't argue with that. He could still feel the anger he had towards her rolling beneath the surface, but it was strangely intertwined with anger at himself, and a need to fix things and make it better for her and better for Nathan. But since he couldn't find the words she needed to hear, the words that said he understood why she kept the secret, he just slowly closed the car door and walked around to the driver's side.

The car ground to life, and he backed out of the driveway. A feeling of déjà vu came over him as they started off looking for Nathan. Again. Only this time, thank goodness, his daughter was safely ensconced at her

Grams', playing cards.

It struck him with the force of a blow to the chest. His *son* wasn't safely tucked away anywhere though. He was out there. Alone and dealing with yet another shock, trying to figure out his life. Clay was mad at Jenny for causing this pain, but he knew he had pushed her into telling Nathan the truth, probably before he was ready to hear it. Because *he* wanted Nathan to know, not because it was the best time for Nathan to find out. He was a selfish jerk. He was just so anxious for Nathan to know the truth. He ached to spend time with him, to get to know the boy better.

"What's he like?" The question popped out before Clay had time to reel it back in.

"Nathan?"

He nodded. Of course, Nathan, what was he like? He had so many questions. What sports did he like? Had he had chicken pox? How old was he when he learned to walk, cut his first tooth?

"He's… kind. Did really well in school until this last year. But I think he can pull his grades back up. Unless…"

"Unless this new curve throws him again." Clay finished her sentence. "We'll help make it right for him. We'll find a way."

"I'm not so sure."

"Tell me more. What sports does he play?"

"Just about everything. Baseball, soccer, basketball.

He loves to go fishing with my dad. Oh, and golf."

"What's his favorite?"

"Probably soccer. The one thing he didn't mess around with this last year. He stayed serious about his soccer. He played varsity this year. He was their high scorer. He didn't let on, but I could tell he was so proud of that."

"Childhood illnesses?"

"You're such a doctor." She actually smiled at him then. "Let's see. He had chicken pox before they were regularly giving out the vaccine for it. At about nine months old. Never seen a more miserable baby. A few earaches. Nothing serious. He was a healthy baby."

"Tell me more about him growing up." Clay was desperate for more information. Anything. Everything. Jenny seemed to tune in to his need.

"He was a happy baby, slept through the night at about a month. He walked at exactly ten months. He was so proud of himself he would take a few steps, clap his hands, and fall down on his bottom." She paused, as if searching for a way to condense an entire lifetime into a few sentences. "Started t-ball at five and picked up the other sports as he went along. Makes good grades in school. At least until this last year. Loves science and math. Reads a lot of books."

Clay watched her face as she talked about her son. It lit up with her love for him, that much was obvious. "What else?" He needed more.

"He had his first crush in first grade. Amanda Carver. She was a student teacher. She broke his heart. He recovered enough to have his first girlfriend his freshman year of high school. She broke his heart, too. He doesn't have a very good track record in the broken heart department."

Neither did his father, Clay thought, but he didn't voice it out loud.

"Likes pepperoni pizza, hush puppies, and vanilla ice cream."

"Those are Danielle's favorite foods, too. Maybe it's a genetic thing." The comment hung in the air between them. Clay broke the tension. "But they sure don't know how to make hush puppies back east, we have to come home for that."

He realized, with a start, that he'd called Comfort Crossing home. Comfort Crossing, Mississippi, the town he'd grown up in, where he'd fought so hard to fit in. The town that always reminded him he came from the wrong side of the tracks. But it *did* feel like home to him, and he was no longer intimidated by the other side of the tracks. He realized it was quite possible the whole "which side of the tracks he lived on" was all in his head, a firm belief that Old Man Delacroix had tried to entrench in his thoughts.

But now he liked being home with Greta. He liked seeing his girls spend time with their Grams. He liked the slower pace of the small southern town, instead of the break-neck pace of Boston. It did feel more like home here than Boston had ever felt to him.

Thinking about Greta and the girls made him ask, "Is Nathan close to your parents or Joey's parents?"

"He's close to Joseph's parents, especially Joseph's father. But my parents? No, not them."

Clay doubted Jenny's parents would even know how to get close to their grandchild, they sure hadn't been very affectionate around Jenny, but he didn't voice that thought either. He'd never seen them touch her, much less give her a hug. There had rarely been any words of encouragement. Jenny had tried so hard to win her father's approval, but she had always managed to fall just short of what he expected of her. Though Clay was pretty sure, now that he was an adult and could figure this out, that Jenny's father would never be completely happy with Jenny, no matter what she did.

Chapter Seventeen

By dawn they had exhausted all the places they could even think to look. Clay had driven Jenny around all night to all the local hang outs, checking back frequently at Jenny's house, looking for the car, checking the answering machine at her house, all the time hearing about his son's life. That part had been good. Really good.

He'd finally suggested they go over to Greta's house and he'd see if he could borrow Greta's car to go to the clinic this morning so Jenny could keep his car. Not that he wanted her out driving around by herself. Her eyes had dark circles under them from exhaustion. Her face held a defeated look, so unlike anything he'd ever seen from Jenny. His Jenny was a fighter. A survivor. *His Jenny?* Where had that come from?

They sat at Greta's worn kitchen table sipping coffee, trying to get enough energy to face the day. The sunrise was breaking across the sky in a brilliant display of pinks and yellows, promising a gorgeous day ahead. But right now, in his exhausted numb state of mind, he didn't believe in the promise the sunrise was thrusting at them.

Greta walked into the kitchen in her faded pink bathrobe. "I thought I heard you come in. You didn't find Nathan?"

"No. We looked everywhere we could think of." Clay set down his mug and rubbed his hand over his day-old growth of whiskers.

Greta took a cup of coffee and crossed over to where Jenny was sitting. She placed her hand on Jenny's shoulder, and Jenny reached up and put her hand over Greta's. "It will be okay. He'll show up. He just needs some time," his mom reassured Jenny.

"But I have no idea where he could have been all night. We didn't find any trace of him, and no one had seen him." Jenny's voice sounded tired. "I don't have a feeling that something is wrong, this time, like he is hurt. I really feel like he's just taking time to be alone and process what I told him, but I still want to find him and reassure myself."

"I have to go into the clinic this morning. Doc Baker left on his vacation. I'm sorry, Jenns."

"I know you do. Don't apologize. I'll keep looking."

"Mom, it's been a long time since I asked this, but could I borrow the car today? I want to let Jenny use mine."

"Jenny, are you sure you should be out driving around? How about I get dressed and take you out? You look too tired to drive."

"I don't want to bother you."

"Jenny, don't you realize? It's not a bother. Nathan is family. We need to find him and help him understand everything."

It hit Clay then. Family. They were all a family. Just like his girls and his mom. Nathan had stumbled into a big family who would welcome him with open arms, if he'd just give them a chance. He wasn't sure where that left Jenny. Feeling like an outsider, probably, and scared she'd lose Nathan. He looked over at Jenny and tried to smile encouragingly at her. She didn't smile back.

A sleepy Abigail came into the kitchen and slipped into his lap. Her hair smelled of sleep and peaches from her favorite shampoo. He actually knew what her favorite shampoo was, something he'd never had to deal with before Claire left. He knew a lot of things about his daughters now, that had just never registered before, or he'd never taken the time to find out. Abigail nodded towards Jenny in an unspoken question of why they were all at the kitchen table this early.

"We were out looking for Nathan. He's missing." Jenny's voice was low. "We kind of had a fight last night. He's mad at me right now."

Clay realized with a start that Jenny was in tune with his daughter's unspoken words these days, too.

Abigail jumped off his lap, spilling his coffee in the process. "Hold on. You okay? Did you get burned?"

Abigail shook her head and rushed over to Jenny and grabbed her hand, pulling Jenny to her feet. "What is it, Abigail?"

Abigail pulled Jenny to the screen door and pointed towards the barn.

"Nathan? He's out there?"

Jenny's face filled with hope for the first time in the hours they'd been searching. Abigail nodded her head emphatically, her blonde curls bouncing in agreement.

Clay dropped the dishcloth he was using to clean up the spilled coffee and stood up. He crossed the distance to the doorway in three quick strides. "Come on. Let's go and talk to him." He took Jenny's hand in his, as much to give her strength, as to get strength from her. He was going out to face his son. His son who knew the truth, that Clay was his father. His heart beat faster and he realized he was possibly as scared as he'd ever been in his lifetime.

* * * * *

Clay slipped through the partially open barn door, still holding Jenny's hand, pulling her with him. The smell of hay and wet wood engulfed her as they entered the dimness of the barn. Greta kept no animals in the barn, except for a stray cat or two. Clay stopped and she bumped into his back. He reached out to steady her while they waited for their eyes to adjust to the low light.

Then she saw Nathan, sound asleep on some blankets in the corner. She took the lead and crossed over and looked down at her son. He looked so peaceful in sleep, his hair tousled and his clothes rumpled. He stirred in his sleep and let out a big sigh. The car keys were on the ground beside him. Jenny reached down and picked them up without a sound. She put her finger to her lip and tugged on Clay's hand. She wanted her son to sleep, to find what peace he could while he could. They'd talk to him when he woke up. She had the keys, so he couldn't go anywhere. They'd just wait for him up at the house.

"Let him sleep." She mouthed the words.

Clay nodded in agreement. They crossed the barn floor and slipped back out into the growing light of daybreak. Jenny looked up as the sunrise hinted at signs of a threatening storm—a portent of the day ahead.

* * * * *

Danielle was sitting at the kitchen table drinking a glass of orange juice when they came back inside. "Dad, what's going on?"

"Where's Grams and Abigail?"

"Abby went up to read, and Grams is getting dressed. Grams said Nathan is in the barn. What's going on?"

Clay pulled out a chair and straddled it, resting his elbows on the back of the chair. "We need to talk."

"Okay." Danielle eyed Jenny, standing by the counter.

"She's staying. It involves her, too."

"Is Nathan okay?"

"He's okay. It's just... he found out some news. He's upset right now."

"What news?" Danielle leaned toward him.

"I don't know how to tell you this." He felt a rush of fear. How would Danielle handle the fact she had a brother? That he had fathered a child before she was even born?

"Just say it, Dad."

Clay took a deep breath and glanced over at Jenny. She was holding herself still and taut. "Nathan is my son."

"He's what?" Danielle pushed away from the table.

"He's my son."

"What are you saying? You and Mrs. Bouchard? Nathan is yours?"

"We dated in high school and, well, Jenny got pregnant."

Danielle looked back and forth, from him to Jenny and back again. "So why didn't you marry her? Why did she marry Nathan's dad? I mean, Mr. Bouchard."

"I didn't know she was pregnant. I had just broken up with her."

"You broke up with her right when she found out she was having your baby?" Danielle looked at Jenny. "Man, that's rough."

"So she didn't tell me about the baby."

"No kidding, Dad. Why would she? She wouldn't want you to stay with her just 'cause of the baby. Who wants that?"

Clay looked at his daughter and was suddenly aware that she, so close to Jenny's age when she got pregnant, could put herself smack into Jenny's shoes and understand her decision.

Danielle turned to Jenny. "Weren't you afraid your parents would kill you? I'd be afraid Dad would kill me, or ship me to a convent or something, if that happened to me."

"Yes, I was afraid of what my father might do."

"That's rough." Danielle shook her head. "Your timing is lousy, Dad." Her eyes held a tinge of reproach in them.

"I realize that now."

"So when did you find out Nathan was your son?"

"Just this week. When he was in the hospital."

"And you just told Nathan?"

"Jenny did. Yesterday."

"Man, he must be upset. All along he thought Mr. Bouchard was his dad? And his dad died? Now this? No wonder he's ticked."

Clay heard the clumping of crutches crossing the wooden porch. He looked up and Nathan stood at the screen door.

"Hey, Nathan. Come in." Danielle called to him.

Clay watched his son slowly enter the room, his eyes flashing with pent up anger.

"Son, come in. We'll talk." Clay pushed up off the chair.

"Don't call me son."

"Nathan…" Jenny took a step toward him, but Nathan backed away, clumsy on his crutches. She dropped her hand to her side and took a step back, giving him some space.

Nathan leveled a stare at Clay. He stood there silently for a moment, his eyes bright with emotion. "So what was it? You just didn't want to be bothered with a kid? Is that it?"

"Nathan, I told you Clay only found out this week." Jenny intervened.

"You're probably just protecting him. He didn't want me." He turned to Clay. "You left my mom when you found out, didn't you?"

"I didn't even know about you until this week." Clay kept his voice low and controlled. He ached with the pain he saw in his son's eyes. "I had just broken up with your mother when she found out she was going to have you."

"So you threw my mom away, too?"

"Son—Nathan, it wasn't like that."

"It wasn't? You broke up with her and left her alone."

"I didn't know about you."

"But you didn't want her. So I'm sure you wouldn't have wanted to be bothered with me." Nathan leaned against the counter, clutching the crutches. "My dad was a great dad. He loved me. I sure don't need someone coming into my life now and bossing me around. You're not my *dad*. Understand me? I have a dad."

"I'm not trying to take his place."

"Because there's no way you can." Nathan shifted and his crutches crashed to the floor. Danielle jumped up and picked them up for him.

Nathan looked him straight in the eyes, with a look so full of anger Clay had a hard time keeping from stepping back—or maybe from stepping forward—to console his son. The pain in his son's eyes was raw.

"I don't need you." Nathan whirled towards Jenny. "And I don't need you either. You lied to me my whole life. I don't trust you. Just leave me alone." He grabbed the crutches from Danielle. "Everyone just leave me alone" He banged out the door.

Jenny stood there silently. She shed no tears, but a look of pure anguish settled across her face. Her shoulders sagged with the weight of knowing the pain her son was in. She turned and faced the window.

"Dad, let me go. I'll talk to him. Why don't you guys just give him some time?"

Clay nodded at his daughter. She slipped out the screen door. His daughter was off to see if she could help his son, a strange turn of events, though at about this minute he was sure nothing would ever surprise him again.

"Jenny, go home and get some rest."

Jenny turned away from the window and looked at him, saying nothing.

"I'm sure Greta will drive Nathan home later. Or he's welcome to stay here. Give him time with Danielle."

"I'll go." Jenny slowly gathered up her bag and keys. "You'll check in with Greta and see how he's doing?"

"I will. I promise. Try to get some sleep."

Jenny stood there looking totally defeated and alone. Her eyes were lifeless. She fingered her keys, as if not sure what she was supposed to do. One part of him so wanted to fix everything for her and one part was still so angry and warned him she'd brought this on herself.

He wasn't very proud of himself, but the anger side won out, and he watched her silently walk out the door.

Chapter Eighteen

Jenny entered the empty house. The sunlight filtering through the window and gently fell across the kitchen chair where Nathan always sat. It mocked her with bright cheerful taunts. She walked through the house seeing where Nathan had messed up the cushions on the couch and left an empty pop can on the coffee table. A pair of his sandals poked out from under a sports magazine. She picked up a cushion from the couch and pressed it to her face. It smelled of Nathan's shampoo and soap. She sucked in a deep breath then gently placed the cushion back where it belonged.

She ached to hold her son in her arms, to make everything better, to somehow get through to him and explain. If she had known seventeen years ago how this would all turn out…

Who was she kidding? She would still have made the same decision. She hadn't believed she had any other options back then. She'd been so scared. Only she was even more scared now, that she'd lose Nathan for good. That she'd never find a way to make this right with him. What if he was so mad at her that he wanted to live with his grandparents? Would that still even be an option? She didn't even know how Joseph's parents would feel about Nathan when they found out the truth. They may never want to see her again, but hopefully they'd still want Nathan in their lives.

What if Nathan got over his anger at Clay, since it truly wasn't Clay's fault, and decided he wanted to live with his father? Her heart twisted. It could very well happen. She might lose the very thing she held dearest in her life.

She couldn't think about it now, no longer able to sort her thoughts out into any logical sequence. She sank down onto the couch.

She picked up the cushion and held it to her chest. She leaned back against the couch, no longer able to move. Even the thought of standing was too much. Everything was just too much. She closed her eyes. She'd just rest a few minutes, that was all.

* * * * *

"Mom, you okay with all of this?" Clay had showered and changed clothes. He'd called Velda and said he'd be late, but he'd be there soon. He'd explained the whole situation to Abigail, about Nathan being his son, and she seemed to take it all in stride and had given him a big hug. Might have something to do with the fact she idolized Nathan already.

"I'll be fine. You go along to work. Nathan is welcome here, or if he wants to go home, I'll drive him."

"Thanks, Mom. I don't know what I would have done without you this week." He pressed a kiss to his mother's cheek.

"How about you repay me by telling Jenny the truth now."

"What do you mean?"

"I mean the truth about why you broke up with her all those years ago. And don't give me any malarkey about wanting your freedom. You were in love with the girl. The real kind of love. You might still be, if you get past your outrage about her not telling you about the baby. You know she would have told you if you hadn't broken her heart and said you didn't want her anymore."

Clay sank down in the chair beside his mom. "I know that. I feel like, in a way, this is my fault. I didn't want to break up with her, you know."

"I know."

"It was her father."

In her typical Greta way, she sat there quietly and let him explain.

"He threatened to disown Jenny if I didn't break up with her. He said she'd not get a dime towards college. That she'd never be welcome in his house again. And..." Clay wasn't sure how his mom would take the next part. "He said he'd make sure you got fired and never taught in the state again."

"That spiteful old geezer. So afraid of losing what he never really had. You should never have worried about me. I would have found work somewhere."

"There was no way, after all you had done for me, I was going to let him take away your job."

"Clay Miller, I'm a survivor. I would have found a way to get by. We could have figured it all out together."

"I wanted more than that for you. You loved teaching. And Jenny... I couldn't stand to see her rejected by her father either. She spent her whole life trying to win his approval. And you know Mrs. Delacroix would never have stood up to the old man. I just couldn't let it happen." He raked his hands through his hair. "I figured I'd get my degree and come back and prove to Old Man Delacroix I was worthy of his daughter."

"You've always been worthy of Jenny. You're a fine man, Clay."

"Well, he had me half convinced I wasn't good enough, from the wrong side of the tracks. That I'd ruin Jenny's life."

"So you told her you didn't love her anymore."

"Biggest mistake in my life."

"You should have trusted her, Clay. A love like you two had is rare. You should have trusted in that love." Greta covered his hand with hers. "You need to tell Jenny the truth now. She deserves that much."

"But her father is so sick. I can't tell her now, when he's

dying."

"Clay, you never give Jenny enough credit. She's a strong woman. She's proven that. Tell her the truth. She needs to know. She'll understand."

"But the timing…"

"There never is a good time to tell a person someone they love has disappointed them. She'll be upset, but I think she's made peace with the kind of man her father is."

"But—"

"No buts." His mom nailed him with a no-nonsense look. "I think you're half afraid of what Jenny is going to say when she finds out you didn't trust her enough to tell her what was really going on. And that your decision to push her away started all of us down this path that led us to where we are today."

Clay knew she was right. He could say he was mad at Jenny… and he was. She'd kept the truth from him for all these years. But he had started them all down this path with his choice to allow Old Man Delacroix to intimidate him, to convince him that he wasn't good enough for Jenny. He hadn't made such good choices in his youth either. His decision had started this whole mess.

Clay leaned over and hugged his mom. "You're right. I'll tell her today."

* * * * *

Jenny woke up curled on the couch with the afternoon sun pouring through the windows. For a moment, she stretched in the luxury of being half awake, half asleep, without any cares cluttering her mind. Then the reality of her life crashed her wide awake. She sat up on the couch and shoved her hair back out of her face with a jerking motion.

She'd shower and go check on Nathan, or at least call Greta. She trudged up the stairs to her bedroom and crossed over to the closet. She glanced up at the top shelf. The memory box. She reached up and pulled it down, needing to be surrounded by the memories. Needing to see the mementos of the time she'd had with Clay. She slowly lifted the lid, wanting to tumble into the world she had shared with him.

Her eyes widened at an envelope placed on top, with Joseph's handwriting scrawled across the front. She slowly opened the envelope and pulled out a letter.

My dearest Jenny,

I am so sorry. I know eventually you will open this box again and see this letter. I have kept this secret all these years, and you deserve to know the truth.

Clay came to me soon after Nathan was born. He told me the truth about why he broke up with you. Your father threatened to disown you and have Greta fired from her teaching job. Had I been a better man, I should have told him Nathan was his son right then. But by then I loved Nathan with all my heart and thought of him as my son. I'm ashamed of my decision. That's why I made you promise to tell him the truth. I hope by now you have told him and the two of you have made your truce. Please forgive me.

I know I was never first in your heart, but I loved the life we had together and I loved both you and Nathan. He was, and always will be, my son.

Joseph

She dropped the paper and sank down on the floor, no longer able to support her own weight. Clay hadn't wanted his freedom. He had broken up with her because of her father. Her very own uncaring, non-approving father. An uncontrollable anger welled up inside of her. How could her father have done this to Clay? To her? To Nathan? He'd set them down a pathway that led to the pain they were going through now, had robbed them of years of being together.

And Joseph. He'd known the truth and kept it to himself. How could he have kept that secret from her?

She laughed a half-hearted laugh. She was one to be mad at anyone for keeping secrets. She could even understand Joseph. After being a father to Nathan for a year and loving the boy as he did, she could see how he couldn't bear to give him up. He'd been so good to her. Marrying her. Raising Nathan. Always taking care of them.

She pressed her back against the dresser and sorted through the pictures scattered around her. She and Clay at the school picnic. A picture of Clay, Joseph, Becky Lee, Izzy, and her, in front of the Magnolia Cafe. A ticket to the school play where Joseph had played a minor character on a dare from Clay. A silver bracelet Clay had given her for her sixteenth birthday. She slipped it on now and smiled. So many memories danced through her head. She dropped the pictures back into the box.

If only Joseph had told her the truth. She stopped herself cold. She was no longer going to play the if-only game, the what-if game. They'd all made their choices. Now they had to live with them and move on. Poor Joseph, carrying this guilt with him all these years, always afraid, in the back of his mind, that he'd lose her or Nathan. She wished she could have assured him that she wasn't leaving him. She wouldn't have, not even if she'd found out why Clay broke up with her all those years ago. Joseph had done so much for her, and she had genuinely cared for him. He was a wonderful father to Nathan. She wouldn't have left him if she had found out all those years ago. She owed him so much. She wouldn't have been able to break his heart, she had actually grown to love Joseph, but he had always known Clay had held a special place in her heart and always would.

She knew why Clay hadn't told her the truth this week either. Because her father was so sick. Clay hadn't wanted her to know what her father had done.

Jenny pushed off the floor with more force than she intended to and knocked over the memory box. That was it. All the secrets needed to be dealt with. She was going to go see Joseph's parents, then her own parents. Then, and only then, she was going to track down Clay and beg him to forgive her, and if he'd let her, she'd spend the rest of her life trying to make it up to him. For what her father had done. For what she'd done. Then she was going to go and right things with Nathan. Somehow. Some way.

Chapter Nineteen

Jenny pulled up to the Bouchards' house. Joseph's parents needed to hear the truth, and they needed to hear it from her. She parked the car alongside the house and took the stairs of the front porch two at a time. She raised the brass knocker on the massive oak door and let it drop. When no one answered, she rang the doorbell. Still no one came to the door. Undefeated, she went around to the back of the house and pushed open the gate to the pool.

Joseph's parents sat out in the open air gazebo by the pool side. They both looked up as she came through the wrought iron gate.

"Jenny, how nice to see you," Joseph's mom, Martha, called out to her. "Come over here. Pour yourself some sweet tea." She motioned to the pitcher of tea on the table. "What brings you out here? Is Nathan all right?"

"He's fine. I just need to talk to the two of you."

Quickly. Before she lost her nerve. She dropped into a chair by the table. "I need to talk to you and I don't know where to start. I've made so many mistakes." Jenny knew her words sounded rushed and her thoughts disjointed.

"Just tell us." Joseph's father leaned forward.

"It's about Nathan. And Joseph." The words just wouldn't come. She didn't know how she could take away their last connection to their son.

"We already know, dear." Martha set down her glass of tea. "Joseph told us about Clay and Nathan, right after he got so sick. He told us he was going to have you tell Clay the truth. He wanted us to know the truth from him. I guess he was afraid of our reaction and was trying to protect you. He said you'd come talk to us when the time was right, but I'll tell you the same thing I told him. It doesn't matter to us. Nathan is our grandson. He always will be."

"Martha's right. It doesn't matter to us. He's our grandson."

Jenny skirted dangerously close to tears for about the billionth time this week. "I thought you'd be angry or you'd feel... I don't know what I thought."

"We're glad Joseph had Nathan in his life. He adored his son. We adore him, too. Nothing will change that. Nothing." Martha reached over and patted her knee. "I guess you've told Clay?"

Jenny nodded. "And Nathan. Nathan isn't speaking to me. He's so angry. He's so mad I lied to him, and I'm sure he feels like he lost Joseph all over again."

"It is unfortunate he's had to deal with all of this at such a young age. But that's life sometimes. It hands us things we just have to deal with in whatever way we can at the time. He'll come around. He's a good boy. He just needs time. He's had a lot of changes to deal with." Joseph's father came over and put his hand on her shoulder. "Send him by here when he's had time to think it all through. We want to reassure him that he'll always be our grandson, no matter what."

"I love the two of you. You know that, don't you?" Jenny choked out the words, so grateful to these two loving people who had been more like parents to her than her own mother and father.

"We know, dear. We love you, too." Martha sat back down. "Have you told your parents?"

"I'm going there right now."

"Good luck, dear." Martha paused for a moment, as if she wasn't sure if she should go on. "You know, you're a wonderful mother. You were a good wife to Joseph. You have a good heart. Don't let your father convince you otherwise."

"Thank you." Jenny took strength from Martha's words and got up and walked out through the gate to face her next hurdle. She was going to confront her father about what he had done.

* * * * *

Jenny sat on the front step of her parents' house, trying to summon the courage to go in and face her father. She sucked in a deep breath and pulled her shoulders up and her back straight. She was going into the lions' den to face her parents, to confront her father. She'd never stood up to her father in her whole life, and wasn't sure she'd know how to do it now. But one thing she was sure of, he was going to know Clay was Nathan's father and she was proud of it. That he couldn't meddle anymore, or pull strings and try and ruin people's lives. He'd played a terrible game of twisting fates. He had had no right to interfere in her life back then. His heartless interferences had cost Clay years of being a father to his son. She pushed up off the stairs, shaking slightly, but she didn't know if it was from anger or if she was that scared to stand up to her father.

She pushed open the wide front door and crossed into the darkened hallway. "Mother? You home?"

Cook came out of the dining room. "Hi, Mrs. Bouchard. Your father is the den. Your mother is upstairs."

"Thank you."

Jenny walked down the hallway to the den, wishing she didn't have to meet her father on his home turf, the sacred den no one was allowed to enter unless he invited them. In a burst of defiance, she pushed open the door to the den with a brief knock, but didn't wait to be invited in.

"Father, I need to talk to you."

Her father sat in an oversized leather chair, the chocolate brown color only adding to the dark oppressive feel of the room.

"What?" Her father looked up. "Jennifer." He did not look pleased at being disturbed.

"We need to talk."

"I'm a bit busy right now." He sat there with a book on his lap, playing his power game of one-upmanship.

"Well, it can't wait." She perched on the arm of another chair, knowing her father couldn't abide by that.

"Take a seat."

"I'm fine right here."

Her father shook his head. "So, what is so important that you burst in uninvited and demand my attention?"

"See, Father, that's part of the whole problem. I'm your daughter. I shouldn't have to be invited. I shouldn't have to demand your time if I say I need to talk to you."

"Jennifer, you're overwrought."

"No, I'm actually quite completely clear right now. I have something to tell you, then I'll leave you alone." She had found the courage now to stand up to this man, to tell him the truth. She felt herself tense up and forced herself to relax. What was he going to do to her now? He couldn't ground her. She was a grown woman.

Her father looked up at her, clearly annoyed. She saw her mother come to the doorway of the den and nod slightly, but didn't say a word to interrupt them.

"It's about Nathan. And Joseph. And Clay Miller."

"What's that Miller boy have to do with anything?"

"That Miller boy is Dr. Miller now. He's a fine man. And he's Nathan's father."

"You're talking crazy now."

"Clay is Nathan's father. Can I spell it out any more clearly for you? You know when you threatened Clay with taking away Greta's job, and you threatened to disown me if he didn't break up with me?"

She heard her mother gasp in the doorway, saw her mother's hand go up to her throat. Amazingly, her mother had entered the room without her husband's invitation either.

"When I found out I was pregnant, I went to go and tell Clay. But he broke up with me first. Said he didn't want me and wanted to be free. Now I found out it was all so you wouldn't disown me and his mother wouldn't lose her job."

"Well, it worked out okay, now, didn't it? Joseph married you, and he was a much more suitable husband than that Miller boy would have been."

"Don't you understand, Father?" Jenny stood up. "You took away Clay's right to be Nathan's father. You threatened a boy that you were going to make sure his mother couldn't find a job. You told him you'd disown me. You had no right."

"He wasn't good enough for you."

Her mother came over and slipped an arm around her waist. "Did you do that? What Jenny said? Threaten that boy and say you'd disown your own daughter?"

"This doesn't concern you."

"It doesn't *concern* me?"

Jenny looked at her mother in awe. She'd never heard her stand up to her father. Ever. Her father was getting shocks from all sides today and she didn't feel one bit sorry for him.

"Jenny is my daughter. Of course this concerns me. How could you threaten to disown your own daughter?"

"It was for her own good. That Miller boy was no good."

"He was a boy with a good heart who loved your daughter."

"Well, she luckily tricked Joseph into marrying her so Nathan could have a proper last name."

Jenny looked over at her father, not liking the man at all. She'd tolerated his attitude and his criticism for too many years. "I did *not* trick Joseph into marrying me. He knew about Nathan. That Clay was his father."

"Then why the heck did he marry you?"

Jenny stepped back. Her heart ached with the realization she would never win her father's approval. No matter what. Then, just as suddenly, it hit her that she no longer really cared if she did or didn't. Why had she spent her whole life trying to twist into the person he wanted her to be? A person she didn't want to be.

She felt her mom's arm tighten around her waist. Jenny slipped her hand over her mother's and squeezed it, then set her sights on her father. "Joseph married me to protect me from *you*. I was so afraid of you then. Of what you'd do if you found I was pregnant and not married. Afraid you'd force me to give the baby away. There was no way I could let that happen. Joseph gave Nathan his name. He kept the town gossip at bay." She stepped out of her mother's arm and walked the two steps to her father's chair. "I'm not afraid of you anymore. Say what you want. Do what you want. I don't care. I'm disgusted you threatened Clay, but I can't change what happened from the outcome. But I will *not* let you continue bad mouthing Clay." She knew her eyes flashed with anger.

"Jennifer, I will not allow you to speak to me that way." He clapped his hand against the arm of the leather chair.

"Father, right now I feel like it would be okay if I never spoke to you again, I am so angry. I'm done trying to please you. So you can accept Clay is Nathan's father, or not. But if you don't accept it, Nathan won't be coming around here to listen to you rant about his father. Is that understood?" Her heart pounded, she clenched her fists, sure in her determination.

"Look here, missy—"

"No, Father. I'm not listening to you anymore. You've lost that right." She shook her head and turned to her mother. "Mother, I'm sorry. I know this puts you in the middle. I don't mean to cause you any pain."

"You have every right to be mad at your father." Her mother turned and faced her husband. "I'm mad at him right now, too. All those years. Threatened a young boy. That was just wrong."

"Don't you start in on me too!"

"Jenny, I'll walk you out." Jenny opened her eyes in amazement as her mother laced her arm through hers and walked her out the door. Her mother pulled the door to the den closed behind them with what could almost be considered a resounding slam.

Jenny heard a big sigh escape her mother. She grinned at her mother then. "It felt kind of good to stand up to him, didn't it?"

The corners of her mother's mouth turned up in a half smile, slightly tinged by shock. "I guess it did." A smile spread across her face all the way, and her eyes danced. "It felt really good." She tugged at Jenny's arm. "Come sit with me for a minute or two."

Jenny went out on the porch with her mother, finally feeling a peace she didn't think was possible in this house. She honestly didn't care if that crusty, cranky, mean-spirited man in the den approved of her or not. It was a huge relief to toss that burden aside after all these years.

"I'm glad you told us the truth, dear. I'd been wondering all this time, but never dared to ask."

"What do you mean?"

"Well, I knew you were pregnant all those years ago,

probably before you did. You'd been sick in the mornings. Then, one day you walked into the kitchen when Cook was frying bacon and you bolted out of there for the bathroom. I was pretty sure then."

"Really?"

"But I thought you had gone to tell Clay and he had broken up with you because of the pregnancy. I couldn't understand that, because he'd always seemed so responsible. I didn't know what your father had done. How he'd threatened him. Or I would have made things right by you and by Clay. I'm so sorry."

"It isn't your fault, Mother." Her heart swelled with this new found connection with her mother.

"Then all of a sudden you said you were marrying Joseph. I knew you didn't love him, but I thought your marrying him would keep your father from knowing about the pregnancy. So that's why I was on your side when you wanted a quick, small wedding. I didn't know you had told Joseph the truth though. And I just couldn't reconcile the Jenny I knew, to the one who would trick a man into believing someone else's son was his own."

"I couldn't do that!"

"I realize that. I was just sorry you were marrying a man you didn't love. It's lonely, spending a lifetime with a man who everyone says is right for you, but you don't love and he makes no pretense of pretending he loves you either."

Jenny looked at her mother through new eyes, ones

that saw how lonely her mother's life had been. Her parents and their separate bedrooms. His father never appreciating her mother except for an acceptable woman on his arm, who knew how to entertain and advance his career. She doubted he even saw her mother as a person in her own right. "I'm so sorry, Mother."

"Ah, don't be. I chose this life. I didn't really know any better. I never had the kind of love I saw you had with Clay. But then you married Joseph and I was so disappointed. I didn't want my daughter to have the same life as mine. But then, as the years went by, it seemed like you came to care about Joseph. You seemed happy."

"I was happy. He was good to Nathan and me. We had a lot of good times. I did love him. He was wonderful to me and to Nathan. We had a good life together. It's just all that time, Clay still had a piece of my heart."

"I'm so glad to find out Clay didn't back away when he found out you were pregnant. I should have known he was a better man than that. It's time to make it right with him. You two lost a lot of years, but you can't change that. You both made a lot of choices that led you to where you are now. You need to see if you have enough love left to try it again, for one last chance at happiness together. True love is worth taking that risk." Her mother stood up and reached for her daughter's hand. "Now, go find Clay and make things right if you can. Then the two of you make it right for Nathan."

Chapter Twenty

When Clay walked into Magnolia Cafe, Becky Lee looked up from the counter where she stood filling up the salt shakers. "Hey, Clay, what brings you here?"

He crossed to the counter and slid onto a round vinyl bar stool. "I'm looking for Jenny."

"Really?" Becky Lee's mouth held a glimmer of a smile.

"What's so funny?"

"Well, she was in here about an hour ago, looking for you."

"She was?"

"Yep, after I made her tell me why she was so all fired up hot to trot to find you." Becky Lee shook her head. "I'm not sure what to do with the two of you. I'll tell you one thing, though, you two deserve each other. You've got a love that survived all these years if you can get past the secrets and the hurt. Love like that isn't something you should just throw away. That kind of love is worth every risk to try and make it work. Told her the very same thing." She punctuated her lecture by plopping the salt shaker down on the counter.

"I've looked everywhere for her. I called Mom, and she's not over there talking to Nathan. I just can't think of where else to look."

Becky Lee raised one eyebrow. "Really? Then you don't know Jenny as well as I thought you did. Maybe you don't deserve her."

"Where is she, Bec?"

Becky Lee shook her head. "Well where do you think she'd go if she's trying to sort everything out in her head?"

Clay leaned over the counter and planted a big kiss on Becky Lee's cheek. "I'm a fool. Of course! I should have looked there first."

Becky Lee just grinned at him and shook her head. "Young love. What's the world to do with it?"

Clay strode out of the cafe and was parking his car beside Jenny's not fifteen minutes later. Of course she'd head to the stream. He should have thought of that first thing instead of chasing himself around town.

He hurried down the pathway, pushing at the branches as they slapped at him as he rushed past. He broke into the opening and saw her, sitting on a rock at the edge of the stream, bare feet dangling in the water, lost in thought.

"Jenns?"

She looked up and smiled like she had known he

would show up there eventually.

"I have to talk to you." He sat down beside her on the rock and noticed the silver bracelet on her slender wrist, the one he had given her all those years ago. He reached for her hand. "I have to tell you something about when we broke up." He wanted to get it all out in a rush before he had a chance to think about it. Knowing it was going to hurt her to find out what her father had done and to find out what Joseph had done, keeping the truth after he found out why Clay had broken up with Jenny. And what he feared most, telling her he hadn't trusted her enough all those years ago to tell her about her father's threats. He hadn't trusted in their love.

"I already know."

"What do you mean?"

"I found a letter from Joseph. It said why you broke up with me. My father threatened you. He also said you came to visit, after Nathan was born, and told Joseph the truth. But he couldn't bear it then. He already thought of Nathan as his own. So he didn't tell you the truth. Didn't tell me the truth."

Clay took her other hand and pressed both of them to his chest. "So many secrets that led us to so many choices."

"Clay, I know you can never forgive me for keeping Nathan a secret from you. I should have told you. I should have."

"Yes, you should have. But I should have believed in

you and not let your father threaten me. I should have trusted in your love." He looked into her eyes. "And, Jenny, I do forgive you for keeping Nathan a secret. I understand. It was my fault, too. For letting your dad threaten me into breaking up with you. I so wish I had trusted in our love back then."

He saw tears chase the corners of Jenny's eyes. "We've made a lot of mistakes. Nathan is paying for them now." Jenny reached up and placed her hand on the side of his face. The warmth spread through him.

"We need to find Nathan and explain and try to make it right for him."

"We do. But what do we say about us? How is this going to work for him? Going back and forth on holidays? How do we work this?" Jenny asked.

"How do you want it to work?" Clay held his breath, waiting for the answer he wanted so badly to hear.

"I know I hurt you when I married your best friend. I know Claire hurt you when she left you for your partner. But I want you to trust me now and know I would never hurt you like that again. I won't ever keep a secret. You need to trust in the fact…" She reached up and brushed the lightest of kisses on his lips. "Trust the fact that I love you. I always have. And I always will."

Clay looked out over the stream for a moment, trying to process everything that had happened in the last few days, trying to sort out his feelings. Trying to let it sink in that Jenny loved him. *Him.* He could take a chance on love, and believe she wouldn't leave him, or he could work out some kind of crazy visitation schedule with his son, always knowing he'd been too afraid to do what he really wanted, to marry his son's mother.

He turned back to Jenny. "I think it's time I made an honest woman out of you, Jenns."

Her face broke into a full beaming smile and she threw her arms around his neck. "I think it's time I made and honest man out of you, Clay Miller."

He bent down to kiss her then, his lips pressing against hers. He wrapped his arms around her, drawing her closer.

"Clay?"

"Hm?" He didn't even pause in his trail of kisses down her neck.

"Would you think me a wanton woman if I said I wanted you to make love to me right now?"

"Yes, I would." He grinned at her. "Have I ever told you how much I enjoy a good wonton woman?"

"No, but you could show me."

"At your service, ma'am." He stood up and reached his hand down to hers. She stood up and slid into his arms. He caught his breath.

"Okay then." He swooped her up in his arms and placed her gently under their willow tree.

"Clay. Now." She pulled him into her arms.

"As you wish." He ended their torturous waiting game. His heart beat in rhythm with hers, finally in sync after all these years, finally trusting in their love.

Chapter Twenty-One

Jenny felt Clay's strong hand on her elbow as they walked up the stone pathway to Greta's house. Nathan and Danielle sat out on the porch. They both looked up and Danielle waved to them.

"Hey, Dad." Danielle smiled tentatively at them as they climbed the stairs.

"Hi, baby." Clay answered.

Jenny looked over at Nathan. He looked calmer now. At least he hadn't bolted the moment he saw them. She still didn't know how to start into it all, what to say to make it better.

"Nathan, would it be okay to talk now?" Clay surprised her by jumping right into the middle of things, but he took a good approach by asking Nathan if it was okay.

"I guess so."

That was more encouraging than Jenny had hoped for.

"We've been talking." Danielle jumped in.

"Yeah, we have. Danielle told me I'm being a jerk."

"I didn't call you a jerk." Danielle stopped him. "I just said I understood how scared your mom must have been back then. That Daddy had just broken up with her, and her father probably would have killed her if he found out."

"I agreed with her on that part, where Grandfather would have killed you."

"Nathan, I am sorry it worked out this way. I know you must feel like I betrayed you." Jenny leaned against the porch railing directly across from Nathan. Clay came and stood beside her, leaning against a nearby porch post. "I just tried to do what was best for you."

"I know that. It just su— It's just hard. I always thought Dad—Joseph—was my dad."

"He was your dad." Clay broke in. "Nothing I can ever do or say will take that from you. I understand he was a great dad to you. I'm glad of that. If I couldn't be there for you, I'm glad it was Joey. He was a genuinely good person."

Nathan looked at Clay with gratitude in his eyes.

"That doesn't mean I don't want to become an important part of your life now, too."

"I can't call you Dad."

"I'll never ask you to." Clay raised one eyebrow. "But I hope you quit calling me sir."

"I could do that." Nathan's mouth held a hint of a smile at the corners, and Jenny's heart soared with the growing hope things were going to work out between Clay and Nathan.

"Now, about your mom."

"I guess you're never going to forgive her, are you?" Nathan held an almost protective look in his eyes.

"I already have. I'm truly sorry I missed all those years with you, but hopefully we can make up for lost time. I hope you can forgive your mom too, and realize she was just doing what she thought was best for you."

Nathan stood up, grabbed one crutch, and hobbled across the porch to her. "Mom, I understand why you did it. And Danielle is right, you were a kid. I know Grandfather Delacroix would have tossed you out to the street, or taken me away. I'm glad that didn't happen. I like you being my mom."

Jenny's whole world fell into place at that very moment in her life. It was like her life had been a jigsaw puzzle she had been trying forever to finish—and she had just found the last piece and snapped it into place. She took her son in her arms and held him. He wrapped his arms around her. Her heart was at peace after all these years. The secrets were over. She smiled over her son's shoulder at Clay.

"I love you, Mom."

"I love you too, sweetheart."

The screen door swung open wide and Abigail and Greta came out on the porch. "I thought I heard your voices." Greta said while she took in the scene.

"Hey, Mom."

Greta looked over at Jenny hugging Nathan. "Looks like things are going just fine out here."

Nathan pulled back and hobbled back to the chair. He plopped down beside a smiling Danielle.

"So, how is this going to work? Am I going to go to Boston for some of the holidays or something?"

Jenny heard Clay take a deep breath. "Well, Jenny and I have made a decision we hope all of you will be happy with."

Greta grinned.

"We're going to get married. There won't be any going back and forth."

"Dad!" Danielle jumped up and clapped her hands. "Married. To Mrs. Bouchard?"

"How about you call me Jenny?"

"Jenny." Danielle said the name as if trying it on for size. "Cool."

Jenny watched while this incredible man she was so totally head over heels in love with turned towards their son. "How about you call me Clay? We can try that out, and go from there."

"That works." Nathan broke into a slow, lazy smile, so like his father's.

"Well, congratulations you two. It's been a long time coming, but I'm glad you finally made it." Greta came up to Jenny and gave her a hug. "Welcome to the family."

"But where are we going to live? In Boston?" Danielle

asked.

"We're going to live in Comfort Crossing. Is that okay with you?"

"I think that's cool. I'm beginning to like it here." Danielle paused and wrinkled her nose. "Well, except for those stupid school uniforms."

Clay laughed. "I already talked to Doc Baker earlier this week. I had hoped we could maybe move here. Doc Baker wants to semi-retire, so I'll take over the clinic, and he's going to stay on part time for a while."

"That's great news, son." Greta looked like she was going to burst with happiness. Her eyes sparkled as she looked around at all the family on her porch. "Great news."

Jenny looked over at Abigail, standing near her sister's chair, looking slightly confused.

"Hey, Short Stuff, come over here." Nathan patted the footstool in front of his chair.

Abigail slowly trudged over to the footrest and sat down. She looked up at Nathan. He reached out and took her hand.

"You cool with this?"

Abigail looked at Nathan with adoring eyes. "D—does this mean you'll be my big brother?" The girl's voice came out slow and clear.

"Abby!" Danielle squealed in delight.

Nathan pulled Abigail into his lap and hugged her. "It sure does, Short Stuff."

Jenny reached out and grabbed Clay's hand. He turned toward her with his just-for-her smile. With a whoop of gratitude, he grabbed her and swung her into the air. Life just didn't get much better than this in Comfort Crossing.

Chapter Twenty-Two

Bella, Becky Lee and Jenny sat on Jenny's wide front porch. The late afternoon sunshine bathed the yard in sweet yellow light. For once, in a very long time, Bella realized that everything was just right in their little world.

"So, you going to have a big wedding?" Becky Lee picked up some fancy pastry thingie that she had brought over.

"Nope. Just you two and family. Because, you know, you guys are family." Jenny smiled.

"You could have it in my backyard. I have that arbor with the roses. It's shaded late afternoon. Or you could use the tea room of Sylvia's restaurant. I think it's going to be fabulous when the renovations are finished." Bella's mind was already planning flowers and decorations. "I could set it all up."

"I don't know, Izz. Clay and I haven't really talked about it much, but either idea sounds wonderful."

"Izzy is always happy with a place to decorate or an event to plan," Becky Lee laughed. "Good thing she's such an expert at it."

"Oh, and I just found this vintage wedding dress, it would be perfect. We could cut it off to knee length. It's simple and so you." Bella reached for one of the pastry thingies. *What had Becky Lee called them?* Didn't matter, they were delicious.

"I wasn't really planning on wearing white."

"Not a problem. I'll dye it any color you want."

"I don't really care where I get married, or what I wear. I'm just glad to finally get to marry Clay."

"We are, too. You guys were meant to be together. It just took a while to get there. I knew you were meant to be together from the first time I saw you and Clay holding hands. You two are like magic together." Becky Lee smiled.

"I feel like I should pinch myself to see if it's all real. I've loved Clay for so many years. Now, finally, we'll be together."

Bella looked at Jenny. She had never looked more content. Her friend deserved a happy ending after all this time. Her heart swelled with joy for Jenny.

"Now, we're going to have to see about Izzy and Owen. How's that going, Izz?" Becky Lee asked.

Good question. How was it going? Owen was out of town a lot and they had been trying to get to know each other this summer when he was in town. He was coming back to Comfort Crossing for most of the next month. Bella was looking forward to seeing where things went with Owen. She felt like a school girl around him. Her heart did a little flip every time she saw him.

Becky Lee looked at her expectantly.

"I'm not sure. But he'll be in town for a while this next trip."

"Good, it will give you more of a chance to get to know him better. I reckon anyone looking at you two can see you're crazy 'bout him, though. " Becky Lee smiled. "He looks a bit smitten with you, too."

"Okay, I admit. I've missed him so much the last few weeks and can't wait for him to be in town for days on end."

"We'll have to all go out when he gets back in town. Introduce him to Clay." Jenny said.

"Oh, I could have you all over for dinner. I love a chance to cook for a crowd." Becky Lee suggested.

"Well, I'm not ever going to turn down one of your meals." Bella smiled at her friend.

"Sounds good to me." Jenny leaned forward, picked up her glass of lemonade, and raised it for a toast. "To things settling down for all of us."

Bella and Becky Lee raised their glasses and smiled.

Contentment washed through Bella. Her friends were happy. She was giddy about Owen coming back in town. Yes, things were just peachy, as far as she was concerned. She watched while a bright red cardinal swooped across the yard, landed on a branch of a large pine tree, and settled into a song. Even the birds were happy today in Comfort Crossing.

THANK YOU for reading *The Memory Box*. I hope you enjoyed it. Learn more about my books and sign up for my newsletter to be updated with information on new releases, promotions, and give-aways at my website, kaycorrell.com

Reviews help other readers find new books. I'd appreciate it if you would leave an honest review.

Comfort Crossing ~ The Series

The Shop on Main - Book One
The Memory Box - Book Two
The Christmas Cottage - A Holiday Novella (Book 2.5)
The Letter - Book Three
The Christmas Scarf - A Holiday Novella (Book 3.5)
The Magnolia Cafe - Book Four
The Unexpected Wedding - Book Five (Summer of 2016)

The books are all part of a series, but each book can be read as a stand-alone story. Jenny and her best friends, Bella and Becky Lee, navigate the heartaches and triumphs of love and life in the small Southern town of Comfort Crossing, Mississippi.

Did you miss *The Shop on Main* - Book One in the Comfort Crossing series?
Sometimes, doing the right thing backfires...

Bella Amaud is desperate when she learns her business and the home she lives in with her two boys are about to be whisked out from under her. As she scrambles to maintain her fragile financial security and independence, she fears she may lose more than just *The Shop on Main* and her home.

Nothing is working out like Bella planned—she finds out the man she is falling for, Owen Campbell, is the businessman at the center of all her problems.

Owen has secretly longed to belong—somewhere— anywhere—his whole life. When he decides to give his long-lost brother, Jake, back his birthright, he unknowingly thwarts his briefly held hope of a place where he can put down roots and a family he longs for.

Nothing is working out like Owen planned—neither Bella nor Jake wants anything to do with him.

How can a man who is used to being in control and a woman determined to make it all on her own find a way to happiness?

The Memory Box - Book Two
Sometimes, mistakes are made for the best of reasons...

When Dr. Clay Miller returns to Comfort Crossing with his two daughters, Jenny Bouchard knows it is time. Time to tell him the truth, no matter the consequences. Clay has a son, Nathan.

From the moment Jenny and Clay see each other again, the attraction still pulsates between them, a fact they both do their best to ignore. Jenny searches for the right moment to tell Clay the truth and a chance to explain— she had made her choice, kept her secret, to protect her son. When Nathan is injured, she knows her time is running out. Jenny fears when the truth is revealed, she will lose not only Clay, but Nathan as well.

But Clay has a secret of his own...

The Christmas Cottage - A Novella (Book 2.5)
A story of love, moving on, and a dog name Louie...

Veterinarian Holly Thompson accepts a temporary position in Comfort Crossing in an effort to escape all things Christmas. What she finds is a small town that embraces all things Christmas and a handsome neighbor with a small son who both capture her heart. Add to that their adorable pup, and she knows the holidays are not going to be what she planned. At all.

Steve Bergeron is quite content being a single father. He's not willing to risk his heart — or his son's — on another woman who is sure to leave them. It's quite clear Holly will be gone by the new year. But he finds himself willing to do anything to chase away the sadness that lurks in the depths of Holly's eyes. This isn't part of his carefully laid out plans. At all.

When an accident on Christmas Eve forces them both to question their choices, can the magic of the season warm their hearts and bring love and joy back into their lives?

The Letter ~ Book Three
Sometimes life offers second chances ...

Madeline Stuart, a St. Louis-based accountant, has sworn off relationships. Reeling from a breakup with her long-term boyfriend and her mother's recent death, she's determined to avoid personal entanglements of any kind.

Deserted by his big-city girlfriend because he's a "country bumpkin," Gil Amaud, a business owner in Comfort Crossing, Mississippi, has sworn off women.

Madeline's curiosity is piqued when she finds an old letter hidden in her grandmother's antique writing desk addressed to Josephine Amaud in Comfort Crossing. With Gil's help, she tracks Josephine down and learns the letter is from her first beau, who disappeared suddenly many years ago.

While they search for Josephine's lost love, both Gil and Madeline try to deny the attraction developing between them.

Can a big-city woman and a small-town businessman help to reunite the star-crossed lovers? And can they find a way to put aside their differences to build a future together in this sweet, heartwarming tale of love and forgiveness?

Maybe, just maybe, a second chance is all they really need.

The Christmas Scarf ~ A Holiday Novella (Book 3.5)

Sometimes, Christmas wishes bring their own special magic...

A woman chasing a life-long dream. A man given a second chance at love. If one wins, the other loses. Does a stranger's scarf hold enough magic to make both their Christmas wishes come true?

Missy Sherwood has always wished for one thing, to be a country singer. After trying to make it for years in Nashville, she returns to her hometown of Comfort

Crossing, Mississippi, feeling like a misfit and a failure. But there's no use in telling anyone the truth just yet— she's here for longer than the holidays, she's home for good. Right?

Dylan Rivers is glad to see his old friend return to town, not only to help him with the children's Christmas pageant, but because her homecoming sparks long-forgotten but never acted upon feelings. But there is no use in acting on those feelings, she's soon to head back to her fabulous career in Nashville. Right?

Then a stranger comes to town and has Missy re-examining her dreams. She gets one final chance, and her life-long wish is within her grasp. Is there really magic in the stranger's scarf, or is it in the power of knowing her heart's true wish?

The Magnolia Cafe ~ Book Four
Sometimes, the past isn't quite what it seems...

Reluctant restauranteur, Keely Granger, wants nothing more than to escape the small town she's lived in her whole life, but her guilt and family responsibilities keep her firmly entrenched in Comfort Crossing, Mississippi.

Lonely photojournalist, Hunt Robichaux, takes a break from his life-is-short, chase-after-your-dreams lifestyle and returns home to help his recently widowed sister and his nephews. But every responsibility he's ever taken on ends in disaster, so he's determined to leave before anyone starts to depend on him.

As Keely and Hunt's relationship develops into a more-than-childhood-friends level, Hunt has to decide if he's been chasing his dreams in the wrong part of the world. But as secrets from their past begin to unravel, Keely reels from the knowledge that everything she's believed to be true is all a lie. A disaster — and the truth — threaten to tear them apart forever.

The Unexpected Wedding ~ Book Five (summer of 2016)

Kay Correll writes stories that are a cross between contemporary romance and women's fiction. She likes her fiction with a healthy dose of happily ever after. Her stories are set in the fictional small town of Comfort Crossing, Mississippi. While her books are a series, each one can be read as a stand-alone story.

Kay lives in Missouri and can often be found out and about with her camera, taking a myriad of photographs which she likes to incorporate into her book covers. When not lost in her writing or photography, she can be found spending time with her ever-supportive husband, working in her garden, or playing with her puppies—two cavaliers and one naughty but adorable Australian shepherd. Kay and her husband also love to travel. When it comes to vacation time, she is torn between a nice trip to the beach or the mountains—but the mountains only get considered in the summer—she swears she's allergic to snow.

Learn more about Kay and her books at kaycorrell.com While there, be sure to sign up for her newsletter to hear about new releases, sales, and giveaways.

CPSIA information can be obtained
at www.ICGtesting.com
Printed in the USA
LVHW091656100919
630592LV00003B/520/P

9 780990 482239